Gay Gaslighting

Family members and religious leaders often invoke "love" as their justification for making the lives of LGBTQ folks difficult. But we've learned how to nurture one another.

In these tales from the author of *Mormon Underwear* and *Gayrabian Nights*, a gay man invites two young Mormon missionaries to watch movies on their day off, offering R-rated and eventually X-rated films for their edification. A man receives a substantial inheritance…on the condition he leave his husband. A customer service rep at a Suicide Center established under a new theocracy "assists" those condemned of homosexuality kill themselves.

A bishop is murdered by one of his congregants for being too "liberal." A lonely wife discovers that her husband of twenty-six years is gay. Two missionaries try to interest men at an adult video store in the LDS Church. Parents tell their son he's ugly from the time they first suspect he's gay, hoping he'll be afraid to date once he becomes an adult.

As the fight to remain free of theocracy intensifies, it's important to understand what we're up against and prepare for the political—and emotional—battles ahead. One way is by telling stories oppressors don't want us to hear.

Praise for Johnny Townsend

In *Zombies for Jesus*, "Townsend isn't writing satire, but deeply emotional and revealing portraits of people who are, with a few exceptions, quite lovable."

Kel Munger, *Sacramento News and Review*

In *Sex among the Saints,* "Townsend writes with a deadpan wit and a supple, realistic prose that's full of psychological empathy….he takes his protagonists' moral struggles seriously and invests them with real emotional resonance."

Kirkus Reviews

Inferno in the French Quarter: The UpStairs Lounge Fire is "a gripping account of all the horrors that transpired that night, as well as a respectful remembrance of the victims."

Terry Firma, Patheos

"Johnny Townsend's 'Partying with St. Roch' [in the anthology *Latter-Gay Saints*] tells a beautiful, haunting tale."

Kent Brintnall, Out in Print: Queer Book Reviews

Selling the City of Enoch is "sharply intelligent…pleasingly complex…The stories are full of…doubters, but there's no vindictiveness in these pages; the characters continuously poke holes in Mormonism's more extravagant absurdities, but they take very little pleasure in doing so….Many of Townsend's stories…have a provocative edge to them, but this [book] displays a great deal of insight as well…a playful, biting and surprisingly warm collection."

Kirkus Reviews

Gayrabian Nights is "an allegorical tour de force…a hard-core emotional punch."

Gay. Guy. Reading and Friends

The Washing of Brains has "A lovely writing style, and each story [is] full of unique, engaging characters….immensely entertaining."

Rainbow Awards

In *Dead Mankind Walking*, "Townsend writes in an energetic prose that balances crankiness and humor….A rambunctious volume of short, well-crafted essays…"

Kirkus Reviews

Gay Gaslighting

Johnny Townsend

Contents

In the Mouth of the Beholder.................................9
Where There's a Will.................................23
The Golden Plunger.................................34
A Plague on Both Your Cheeks.........................38
Smoking Beer and Drinking Marijuana...................49
Suicide Center #212.................................63
Lending a Hand…and Other Body Parts.................74
The Coroner's Coronary.................................86
Twenty-Six Years.................................108
Counting Nozzles.................................125
Tilly the Barbarian.................................145
The Mission President's Son.........................172
Bi the Wayside.................................189
Entering at the Rear of the Temple.....................199
P-Day Porn.................................216
Books by Johnny Townsend.........................227
What Readers Have Said.........................240

In the Mouth of the Beholder

"I'm so sorry, Todd," his mother said, patting his arm gently. "I gave you such bad genes."

"I'm in perfect health, Mom," Todd replied.

"Yes, but you're so unattractive."

Todd caught his breath. It wasn't the first time anyone in his family had said this. In fact, they said it all the time these days, but that still never removed the sting. They'd all started pointing out Todd's physical limitations when he announced three months ago on his twenty-first birthday he was finally ready to start dating.

Well, come to think of it, they'd begun making a few comments not long after after he returned from his mission, perhaps after he'd said something nostalgic about missing the camaraderie of other men. But the comments had intensified greatly over the past few months.

"You're old enough to handle the truth, dear," his mother had said during a family council.

As a teen, Todd had often wondered if he was good looking or not. He'd stare at the mirror and try to guess what he'd think if he met himself on the street. But it was impossible to tell. Some days, he looked decent, and other days, he looked awful. So which was it?

Todd was afraid the only reason he ever considered his reflection attractive was simply because he was so used to seeing himself that the horror of his visage had dissipated. Or perhaps people always instinctively approved of their own appearance.

There were folks like Karen Carpenter, of course, who saw something different in the mirror than what actually existed, but those were people with various forms of mental illness. Surely, a normal person would feel an innate sense of acceptance. That had to be the only reason Todd didn't shudder when he looked in the mirror.

But Todd wasn't acceptable, and he should have shuddered. "A guy at school smiled and winked at me the other day," he said. "*He* thinks I'm good looking."

"Oh, Todd," his mother went on, "did he actually *say* that?"

No, Todd thought, he didn't. But one didn't just blurt things like that out. He'd done so himself for the first time last week, two days before meeting the winker, and the man had frowned deeply and walked away.

Maybe the guy already had a partner.

"You need to find a homely girl at church and get married in the temple. You need to have kids of your own. That's what Heavenly Father's plan is for you."

"I need to inflict my ugly genes on more kids?"

Todd's mother shrugged. "It's all about love," she said. "I still love you despite your looks. You'll love your children, too. And in the resurrection, they'll be attractive. Just like you'll be someday after you die."

At that moment, Todd's sister Joanne walked into the kitchen. She was nineteen, already as far along in school as he was because she hadn't gone on a full-time mission that put her behind two years. She looked at her brother sadly and put her hand on his shoulder.

"You know what Mom's saying is true," she said. "Can't you feel the Spirit testifying to you? I'm sorry, but it's best to face facts. No guy is ever going to want you."

It had taken a great deal for Todd to face his homosexuality and accept it after so many years of struggle. He'd been home from his mission over a year now, still living with his parents while he attended the University of Washington. Coming out had been immensely liberating, but within days, Todd's euphoria dissolved as his family kept pointing out he had absolutely no chance for happiness.

"Mom thinks you should try to find a nice girl in the Single Adult group," Joanne continued. "But I think it's best if you just accept the fact you'll always be alone." She now began rubbing her brother's back. "You didn't even want to date in high school. You're lucky. Celibacy comes easy for you."

Todd thought of all the times he'd masturbated during those years while fantasizing about his track coach.

"That's right," his mother agreed. "You really are almost like a girl in that regard." She glanced over at Joanne. "Your looks are just a backup. Heavenly Father wants to make it as easy as possible for you to avoid sin. He *loves* you."

Don't do me any favors, Todd prayed, glancing upward. "So why did God make me gay?" he asked.

With friends like these…

Todd's mother sighed and looked at his sister, who shook her head in response. "Heavenly Father always tests those he loves. He gave us you, didn't he?"

"Okay, Mom," Todd said with a sigh. "I'll go to the Singles dance tonight."

His mother smiled at his sister.

Todd spent the rest of Saturday afternoon studying in his room. He was taking a film course, and one of his "free" movie choices was *Sister Act*. His assignment was to point out a serious flaw in the film. His professor said that almost all movies had at least one flaw in logic, and the students would be better critics or filmmakers if they learned to spot them.

Todd was writing a short paper pointing out that the whole reason Dolores was in hiding was because she was the lone innocent witness to a murder. And yet at the conclusion of the movie, the murderer plans to shoot her in front of fifteen innocent witnesses. Whether or not he was in trouble before, he surely would be now.

When Todd finished typing his paper, he logged onto the Internet. He'd heard people at school mention things like PFLAG and the Human Rights Campaign, but while he was living at home, he had to abide by his parents' rules. They blocked any websites addressing homosexuality in particular or simply sex in general.

Anti-Mormon websites were blocked, too, and even Facebook because it might lead to "inappropriate" socializing. He read a couple of articles on Breitbart and then logged off.

Todd's degree was going to be in English, which meant at best he'd be a teacher. It was going to take a long time after he began working to save up enough money to pay for plastic surgery. But at least he wasn't incurring any student loan debt. His father was paying for his education. He was lucky in everything except looks.

He wondered if ugly people could have sex. He closed his eyes, thinking of his favorite missionary companion. Back in Ireland, Todd used to fantasize they were married. Even now, he wondered what would happen if he picked up the phone and asked if he visit his former companion in Boise.

He wasn't really after sex, though, despite his almost daily fantasies. What he wanted was love. But who in their right mind would want to saddle themselves with someone like Todd for the next forty or fifty years?

Perhaps it would've been better if he still hated his homosexuality the way he was supposed to. Todd couldn't understand why Heavenly Father had let him come to terms with it in the first place. Was it because he'd been doing too good a job dealing with his celibacy before? Maybe God needed to ratchet up the pressure a notch.

If it was a test, though, it seemed Heavenly Father was defeating the purpose if he made it impossible for the young man ever to commit the sin he wanted. Where was the triumph in accomplishing something you didn't have any choice in accomplishing? It was like saying, "You were born! Good job!" Todd had very little to do with it.

"I'm going for a walk," Todd announced, heading for the door.

"Be back in time for dinner," his mother replied.

They lived in the Fremont neighborhood, so it took a couple of buses before Todd arrived on Capitol Hill. He'd overheard guys talking about meeting men in Volunteer Park, and he absolutely needed to talk to another gay man. Well, wanted to, he supposed, not needed to. It was misting outside, so he wasn't sure how many guys would be out, but if Todd wanted the contact enough to come, hopefully some other men might, too.

Todd walked slowly, eying the few guys also walking around the park, their hoods up and their hands deep in their pockets. No one seemed to notice him. He realized they must have learned at some point how to look out of the corner of their eyes to appraise someone without being noticeable. These guys thought he was too ugly to look at directly.

Todd could feel the Holy Ghost bearing witness to him that it was true.

He stepped off the path and began wandering through the rhododendron bushes, not blooming this time of year but their leaves still deeply green. The temperature usually dropped to the mid-thirties most nights in the winter. Todd wondered if he should just come here and sleep outdoors one night and let himself freeze to death.

He had no life worth living if he was always going to be alone. And hadn't he heard the bishop say one day in Sacrament meeting that "it would be better to be dead than gay"?

Todd could keep living with his parents, he supposed, even after he graduated in a couple of years. That might provide *some* company, and it would ensure he remained a virgin. He stopped to lean against a tree. He could feel the cold seeping through his jacket.

"Hi," said a voice next to him. Todd jumped and the man laughed. "Didn't mean to sneak up on you," he said. "It's little cold today, but at least it's not raining."

Was the guy gay, Todd wondered? He looked perfectly normal. "I like the mist," he replied, "but it sure does a number on my glasses."

"So take off your glasses."

Todd took them off and put them in his coat pocket.

"You look pretty good without your glasses," the man commented.

He *was* gay! But if he was here in the bushes, all he was after was sex. "My name's Todd." He held out his hand.

The man took it. "Carson," he said in return.

The man was almost thirty, way too old for him, but Todd found it impossible not to keep chatting. Carson was a radiologist at Group Health on 15th, just a few blocks away. He was originally from Spokane but liked Seattle better. His favorite singer was Etta James, his favorite author Jane Austen. He liked dinosaurs but only the herbivores.

Listening to him reminded Todd of the speed dating activity they'd had with the Single Adult group last month. Only *this* was actually kind of fun. Carson told him his favorite color was taupe (yikes!) and his favorite planet Jupiter (people had a favorite planet?) He said he had a dog but didn't bring her when he was out cruising.

"Cruising?" asked Todd.

"What we're doing right now."

"That's slang for 'talking'?"

Carson laughed and put his hand on Todd's chest. Todd's heart started beating faster, but he doubted the man could tell through a coat, shirt, and garments.

He felt his penis stiffening. Would his garments protect him?

"You sure are good looking," Carson said, touching Todd's cheek with his fingertips. "I've always wanted to meet someone outdoors. It seems so nasty meeting someone in a bar or by sending dick pics online. But I never thought I'd meet someone as attractive as you."

Todd immediately felt himself going flaccid. How could a person feel excited by someone who was clearly lying? It was like hearing, "Wow, you're hung like a horse!" when your dick was only three inches long. Dishonesty was such a turnoff.

At best, he was giving Todd a line. At worst, he was coming on too strong. Every horrible dating scene from every movie Todd had ever seen seemed to flash before his eyes.

"I have to go," he said.

"What? Why?"

"No one's ever going to want me for a husband."

Carson stepped back and frowned. Todd started walking away. "I'm here most Saturday afternoons," he called after him. "Sundays, too."

Which only confirmed he was a slut. If Todd's only options were promiscuity and celibacy, he was most definitely going to choose celibacy.

He arrived back home just in time for dinner. His father said the blessing as usual, and his mother fussed to make sure the rest of the family had everything they needed. She'd baked homemade potato rolls tonight. Joanne talked about this week's Institute lesson, his father talked about taking them all to Disneyworld in the summer, and his mother talked about one of her Visiting Teaching sisters who was always so difficult to reach.

"A man told me I was attractive today," Todd said.

Everyone stopped eating. Todd noted with grim amusement that the dinner table looked like a scene from that commercial with the woman talking about her intestinal problems while everyone on the boardwalk near her freezes.

His mother was the first to recover. "Oh, sweetie," she said, "he was only lying out of pity."

"No one thinks you're attractive," Joanne agreed. "He was probably just desperate. Gay men so often are."

I remembered the poem by John Donne where he tries to seduce a woman by pointing out their blood was already mingled because they'd both been bitten by the same flea.

"You didn't…engage with him, did you, son?" his father asked. Todd knew perfectly well what he meant.

"I would never do such a thing."

Todd could hear a collective sigh, and everyone resumed eating. As his father took a bite of his pork chop, Todd thought about carnivores. And herbivores.

The film *Jurassic Park* came to mind, and the scenes where it differed greatly from the book. In the movie, the paleontologists know all sorts of things they couldn't possibly know. Ellie Sattler knows a certain variety of extinct plant is poisonous, as if one could ever discover such a characteristic by looking at seventy million-year-old fossils.

Alan Grant knows that velociraptors hunt in packs, that *Tyrannosaurus rex* can only see objects if they move, both things it would be impossible to assess from the fossil record alone. One of the main points of the book was that only when people had the actual living dinosaurs in front of them could they really understand what the creatures were like.

Maybe Todd could write a second paper for film class and see if he could get extra credit. If he was going to live alone the rest of his life, he needed to have *something* else to care about.

After dinner, he went to his room and studied his priesthood lesson for the following morning. It was on polygamy.

Heterosexual men could have multiple sex partners throughout eternity, but a gay man couldn't even have one.

Heavenly Father wasn't very nice, Todd realized.

But he was the guy in charge, so Todd took a shower and changed into some pressed slacks and a bright blue dress shirt. Around 8:00, he drove to the stake center with Joanne for the Single Adult dance. She was wearing a sleeveless knee-length green dress, with a green shirt underneath to cover her shoulders. About fifteen women were already in the gym, talking to each other in small groups. Joanne quickly joined one of them. Perhaps eight or nine men milled about the refreshment table.

Todd's friend David came over to shake his hand. "Glad to see you're still trying to be straight," he said.

"I'll never be straight," Todd replied. "I'm trying to stay Mormon."

"If you left the Church, where would you go?" David laughed.

Todd danced with Emily, Heather, and Marina. None of them looked very excited to accept his request, but he'd found that Mormon women rarely turned down a dance invitation. Emily in particular seemed to use the opportunity to show other guys dancing near them how well she could move. She didn't look at Todd more than twice the entire song.

He wondered what it would be like to marry someone he wasn't attracted to, who was also not attracted to him.

Celibacy couldn't be as miserable as that.

By 9:30, Todd had stopped asking girls to the dance floor. David came over and almost put his hand on his shoulder. "You okay?"

"I'm going to make it to the Celestial Kingdom," he said.

David blinked. "Sure you are." He looked at a young woman walking past wearing a hot pink blouse, who'd just arrived in the gym. "Sure you are."

"But I don't feel like dancing anymore."

"That's okay, buddy." He slapped Todd on the shoulder now. "There will be other dances. And we have that Single Adult conference coming up. Don't sweat it." He ran after the woman in the pink blouse.

Joanne seemed to be having a good time, so Todd stayed until the dance ended at 11:00. Then they climbed into his car and headed home. "You need to try a little harder," she said. "Once you're married, you can always have sex in the dark so your wife doesn't have to see you."

Todd stopped at a Stop sign.

"Or you can make love to her from behind so she doesn't have to see your face." Joanne suddenly clapped her hand over her mouth. It wasn't until she did so that Todd realized the same conditions would apply to any man he wanted to be with. A flaw in logic. His sister must have realized the same thing. "You know," she added quickly, "men are a lot pickier about looks than women."

"Yes, I know."

Back at the house, Joanne went to the bathroom to wash off her makeup. Todd sat in the kitchen and poured himself a glass of milk. As he was sipping it, his father walked in and sat in the chair beside him. "Did you have a good time tonight?" He looked uncomfortable, and Todd pitied him for having to deal with a gay son. The man hadn't signed up for this.

"Not really," Todd replied. "But it's okay."

His father reached over as if to put his hand on his Todd's arm, stopped, and returned his hand to the table in front of him. He stretched to peer down the hall to see if anyone else was heading for the kitchen. "I have to tell you something," he said softly, leaning toward his son, "but you have to promise not to let the others know."

"Okay."

His father looked Todd in the eyes, glanced down the hall once more, and returned his gaze to his son's face. "You're not ugly," he said. "We just thought destroying your self-confidence would keep you from trying to find another man. We all made a pact."

Todd set his milk on the table and twisted the glass around and around for the longest time. He thought about all the times the Book of Mormon warned against secret combinations.

A minute passed. Then two. "You okay, son?" his father asked. "I—I want you to be okay."

"Thanks, Dad," Todd said, giving him a weak smile. "I'm going to be fine."

His father smiled in return and stood up from the table. "I'd better get to bed so I'll be able to get up in time for church."

"Goodnight, Dad."

Todd drank the rest of his milk and set the empty glass in front of him, looking at the thin film of milk left behind.

It was funny, but part of him had suspected all along what his family was doing. And yet, even hearing the truth now, Todd could feel it was going to take some time before he ever felt very desirable. He didn't even know what to do to achieve that, though he knew it certainly meant not going to priesthood meeting in the morning.

But he did know where he'd be tomorrow afternoon.

Where There's a Will

"And to my son, Ross, I leave my house in Highland Park." Ross listened to the attorney read his father's will. Astin was here by his side. They'd been together eight years, legally married for three, but Ross was growing a bit tired of him. Tired of marriage in general, really. Still, he couldn't deny that at times like this, it felt good to have someone by his side.

"Ross may only obtain and keep ownership of the house under the following conditions: he must divorce his husband, he may not cohabitate with any male ever again, he may not have a partner relationship with any male who lives at a separate residence, and he may not attempt to sell the house."

Astin jumped up from his seat, and Ross gasped audibly. Could his father legally make such stipulations? Once the house was his, wasn't it his to do with as he pleased?

"My son Ross is blind to the light of the gospel, and I will offer him the iron rod that leads to happiness, if he will but grab hold of it and make his way through the darkness to the tree of life."

Oh, brother, thought Ross. He pulled Astin back into his seat.

The attorney went on to read about a significant trust established to pay for a private detective to keep tabs on Ross at strategic but unannounced intervals to make sure he abided by the rules of the inheritance. If Ross did violate the terms, the house would immediately be donated to his father's favorite anti-abortion group.

The attorney read the rest of the will. Since Ross's mother had died when he was three, he was an only child, and the other items in the will were donated to people other than Ross. A collection of books to this brother, a painting to that sister, his car to that friend. And the $400,000 left over in savings and stocks to the LDS Church.

"As soon as your divorce is legal," the attorney said when he'd finished, "you may take possession of the house."

"You little motherf—" Astin began. Ross put his hand on Astin's arm.

"Let's go," Ross said. They stood and walked to the door. Astin left first, and as soon as his husband was out in the hallway, Ross turned toward the attorney and lifted his right hand to his face, thumb to his ear and pinky finger to his mouth, making a silent gesture to show he would call later. The attorney nodded, and Ross followed his partner into the corridor.

The two men were silent as they drove back to Elgin. When they arrived at their apartment, though, Ross began to speak. "You could always get a sex change," he said.

"You'd want to stay married to me as a woman about as much as I'd like to be one." Astin's lip curled.

"Just thought I'd give you some options."

"You're not seriously thinking about accepting those terms, are you? Geez, Ross, I know we've had our problems…"

Ross thought about all the times Astin had cheated on him, though they'd agreed to a monogamous relationship. He thought about the time he caught Astin reading his journal. He thought about the times Astin didn't have the money to pay his share of the rent, but how he always seemed to have money to fly off for a week to visit his mother.

"At least *I* have a relationship with *my* parents," he'd say.

He thought about the time Astin had given him a dart board and darts for his birthday, the picture on the dart board one of Ross's father. He thought about the time when he had a kidney infection, and Astin promised to give him one of his own kidneys if it came to that.

He thought about the time Astin got drunk at a party and told everyone Ross had a little dick.

"Don't you want to be free of me?" Ross asked. "You certainly seem to be looking for someone else all the time."

"That's just sex," Astin insisted. "I don't love any of those other men."

"Not even Kenneth?" asked Ross. Astin and Kenneth had dated for more than three months before Ross found out. The man had even accompanied Astin on one of his trips to visit his mother.

"No other man is as sweet as you."

A lovely sentiment, Ross wondered, or a blatant attempt at manipulation? "Why don't you go out with some of your friends tonight? I've got a lot of thinking to do."

Astin looked as if he were about to say something but instead nodded and grabbed his car keys. After he left, Ross sat down on the sofa and turned on the stereo, listening to a CD of Il Volo. Two songs later, he switched it off. He needed absolute silence to make his decision. He now lived thirty-five miles away from Chicago, where he worked collecting water bill payments with the Department of Finance.

Highland Park was ten miles closer the city and in a better neighborhood. His father had kept the 1875 Italianate house in perfect condition, so it wouldn't be a money pit, at least not for several years. Of course, the property taxes would be high, so the bottom line was he might end up spending more on taxes and insurance than he currently did on rent.

But wouldn't it be nice not to have to depend on someone else all the time? Especially someone who wasn't very dependable.

Ross was forty-five years old, not over the hill by any means, but he had to admit that one of the reasons he'd never cheated on Astin was because the desire simply wasn't there. He could admire a good-looking man, but he rarely ever felt any lust stirring within his loins. His testosterone level checked out okay. He hadn't even come out as gay until he was twenty-eight, still a virgin. Sex simply had never been that important to him.

Maybe it was okay to give in and agree to celibacy. Not that he cared what Mormons thought of him. He was way past that. And he was convinced his father's spirit wasn't looking down upon him from "the Other Side." He knew there was no other side, no father to appease. Even if there were, the will hadn't specified he could never have sex again, only that he couldn't have a partner. So even if he agreed to the terms and did still get the urge, he wouldn't lose the house.

Astin came back home around 11:00, long after Ross was in bed. "Really?" asked Ross. "On a school night?" Astin taught the fifth grade.

"I wanted to give you some space."

"Beer will do that."

"Aw, honey, I only had three."

"Good night, Astin."

"Sweetie, I'm all loose now from the beer. You may as well take advantage while I'm not tight."

Ross was sure that if Astin's sphincter was relaxed, it was because it had already seen some action that evening. But he thought he'd better go ahead and agree, since the opportunity might soon be gone forever. "Let me get some lube," he whispered.

"Use spit," said Astin. "It hurts a little more that way."

"Really?"

"Makes you seem bigger."

Sheesh. Even when his partner was trying to bribe him, he couldn't help slipping in an insult. Ross used as little spit as possible and forced his way in quickly.

"Unh."

"Feel good, baby?"

"Unh. Yes. Unh." But he was snoring lightly before Ross even managed to come. Ross rested his head on Astin's neck and tried to fall asleep while still lying on his partner's back. He'd miss skin.

In the morning, Ross awoke to the smell of bacon. He put on his boxers and plodded sleepily into the kitchen. "What's the occasion?" he asked.

"We might not have many more mornings together."

"Did you make my lunch, too?"

Astin pointed to a reusable insulated bag on the counter. "Ham, cheese, and bacon sandwich," he said.

Ross's favorite. He wondered how long he could milk his decision as a way to keep Astin behaving nicely. Wouldn't it be lovely to have a devoted husband? Or just as wonderful, no one to hurt him any longer? All day at work, his coworkers had to snap him back to reality. He kept fantasizing about a life without Astin.

In some ways, it seemed the more enviable choice. No more crab infestations. No more waking up in the morning to discover a discharge. No more feeling hurt to realize he was never going to be enough to satisfy another man.

But it also meant Christmas alone. And Thanksgiving. And every other important event. No one to share his stories of annoying customers with. No one to watch *American Horror Story* with.

No one to wake up alongside in the morning.

Astin had dinner ready by the time Ross returned home. "Chicken cacciatore," Ross noted upon entering the kitchen. Another of his favorites.

"And cannolis for dessert."

"Cannoli is already plural."

Astin laughed. "That mission of yours to Sicily wasn't for nothing," he said. Normally, he bristled whenever Ross corrected him. Which really wasn't very often. It was much more likely that Astin would correct him. Even though it was Astin who said things like "tropical steroids" or used the word "epipens" when he meant epicenter.

Could one miss malapropisms?

When it was time for the cannoli, Astin picked one up and shoved his penis into the cream. His penis now looked like a cannolo. "What in the world are you doing?" asked Ross.

"Eat it," Astin commanded.

Ross felt a twitch in his pants and leaned forward to start licking off the excess cream from his partner's penis, nibbling away at the pastry. When he'd finished every last morsel, Astin began pumping away into Ross's mouth, finally coming with a large groan.

"Which cream was better?" Astin asked with a grin.

"The whipped cream," said Ross, "but yours was a close second."

Astin frowned. "Maybe you weren't paying close enough attention. We should do the taste test again." He slipped another cannolo around his penis, and they reenacted their earlier behavior.

It wasn't as exciting the second go around. But this time, Ross conceded that Astin's cream was superior. Astin smiled and headed off to the bathroom. Ross smiled, watching him go. But his smile faded as he realized that not another week would go by before his partner cheated on him again. Even under threat of divorce, he wouldn't be able to stop himself.

The next morning, Astin scrambled some eggs for Ross and prepared his lunch again. After he brushed his teeth, Ross went back out to the kitchen where Astin was washing dishes. He put his hand on Astin's arm. "I've decided," he said.

Astin looked at him, and his face fell. Ross told him what had to be said and then headed out to the car. A huge weight had been lifted off his chest. It was like strapping weights around his ankles for exercise. After walking two miles, he hardly noticed anymore, until he came home and took them off. Then he felt lighter than air.

The weight on his chest had weighed more than five pounds.

When Ross got to work, he looked up the attorney's phone number and gave him a call. "I'm divorcing Astin," he said. "I'll send you copies of all the papers as I get them." He felt content all day, handling even the angriest customers with a smile. He was free. Free! It felt even better than coming out of the closet had all those years before.

People forgot how great freedom was. They were tied down to miserable jobs, unpleasant spouses, an extra thirty pounds, trying to win the affection of their children after divorce, whatever. Didn't people realize how important it was to be free?

When Ross arrived home that evening, Astin had already moved his clothes and other belongings out. He'd left their shared belongings—the furniture and artwork and kitchenware. But even the photos of him were gone from the bookshelves. It was as if he'd never been there.

Except for that lone bottle of Rid still in the medicine cabinet.

A couple of months later, after the divorce was final, Ross walked through his father's Victorian home, every detail in perfect shape. He wished he could make it a museum filled with artifacts of gay liberation. He wished he could turn it into a library filled with books on secular humanism. But what he *had* decided to do would work just as well.

The following week, he knocked on Astin's door. His ex was staying in a fleabag apartment in the worst part of Elgin. In some ways, it was exactly where the man belonged. But as soon as the door opened, Ross got down on one knee. He took Astin's hand. "Will you marry me?" he asked.

Astin laughed. "I wasn't sure you were coming back like you said you would." He got down on his knees as well. "Did it work?"

Ross nodded. "The will never said I couldn't *give* the house away. The Himalayan Cataract Project has possession now. It's on the market for $850,000."

"I can't believe it."

"They'll be able to perform over 33,000 cataract surgeries in Third World countries with that money."

"I love you," Astin said.

"So is that a yes?" Ross asked. "Can we get married again?"

"Yes, yes, yes!" Astin leaned forward and kissed Ross on the lips. After a few moments, their knees began to hurt and they slowly stood up, still locked in a kiss. "We'll just have to wait a couple of weeks," he said, a little too casually.

"Why's that?" asked Ross.

"We want the antibiotics to have time to kill the gonorrhea first, don't we?" He paused a second and then added, "Oh, honey, don't get flustrated."

Ross looked at Astin, so beautiful and appalling and wonderful and awful. Not exactly what he'd always wanted, but perhaps the only thing a husband could be. Any shortcoming Astin had as a person would necessarily be annoying and disappointing, whether it was sexual or financial or intellectual or whatever, as annoying as his own shortcomings were to Astin.

He reached into his pocket and fished about for a moment, pulling out a condom. "I suspected as much," he said. "So I brought a non-lubricated condom and a mouthful of spit."

Astin smiled. He stood back and motioned for Ross to enter the apartment. Ross came in and closed the door, pushing Astin gently up against it and pulling down his pants. He slipped on the condom and pressed his penis against his partner's ass. He pushed himself in as deeply and quickly as he could.

But he didn't use any spit.

The Golden Plunger

There it was. The first trap. Dad had even labeled it. On a metal folding chair next to a snow-covered fir sat two thermoses, with a 5x7 index card taped to the back of the chair. "Trap Number One."

Dad was nothing if not subtle.

Barry trudged through the snow toward the chair. His father had warned him last week about the upcoming test, waiting until the forecast predicted a winter storm before placing the traps, leaving the snow to cover his tracks. "You have to forge your own path through life," Dad had told him time and again.

Barry looked at the two thermoses. He could only drink from one, and he knew his father would verify if he'd chosen correctly. He held up the first thermos and inspected it for clues. The container was stainless steel, showing no other writing besides the name of the company that produced it. The second thermos was black with a stainless steel rim. The company name was NRG.

Energy must mean caffeine, Barry decided. And stainless steel was boring to look at. Since "Choosing the Right" was often boring, he unscrewed the lid to the first container, closed his eyes, and took a deep sip.

Hot chocolate.

He'd made the right decision, avoiding the coffee. Barry smiled as he headed deeper into the woods behind his home. He knew chocolate contained caffeine, too, much less than coffee, of course, but Dad was always telling him it was never permissible to allow *any* degree of sin into his life.

Barry remembered that his father was left-handed and so on a hunch veered left, realizing with a bit of melancholy the man would never know his son as well as his son knew his father. Barry walked carefully through the trees for another few minutes before coming upon the second trap.

Two more thermoses. He walked up to the folding chair and stared downward.

Barry would be turning twelve in August, and the new rules allowed him to be ordained in January of the year he reached deacon age. Dad had wanted him to wait until his birthday anyway, but the cancer diagnosis changed all that.

"You'll have to be the man of the house," Dad told him. "Mom can go back to work and earn a paycheck, but she won't have the priesthood. That means it's up to you to keep our family faithful."

Barry remembered the time his father stood up in Testimony meeting and told the congregation about his recent flight to a work conference. "There was terrible air turbulence," his father had said. "People were shouting and crying, but I just sat in my seat and prayed. And you know what? We landed safely." His father had wiped a tear from his cheek as he continued. "I know Heavenly Father put me on that plane so a righteous man with the priesthood would be on board to keep everyone safe."

Barry kicked the folding chair before him, making one of the thermoses fall to the ground. He didn't know if the anger he felt was over his father abandoning him or the renewed pressure to "be a man." He didn't want to be a man.

The thermos on the ground was light purple, easily visible even half covered with snow. The thermos remaining on the chair was a dull, sage green.

Which was the right container?

On the one hand, green could indicate green tea, and Dad always said that no variety was acceptable. Ever. On the other hand, lavender was clearly not the color for a boy about to be ordained.

How these were supposed to be true tests of character, he'd never understand.

Barry remembered a few months back when the bishop had awarded Kirk, one of the deacons, a replica sword in front of all the youth, its handle bright gold. Kirk had apparently done well in some contest during a father-son camp-out. Then the bishop asked Barry's sister, Samantha, to the podium. She was a Beehive and had also apparently performed successfully during an event at Girls Camp.

Barry had watched as the bishop handed his sister an industrial size plunger covered in gold paint.

Everyone had laughed. Except Barry.

He reached down into the snow and picked up the lavender thermos. His eyes darted between the green and the purple for fifteen seconds, thirty, forty-five. Then he unscrewed the lavender lid, took a deep breath, and drank.

Tea tasted rather odd, Barry thought. He wasn't sure he liked it.

He took another long sip.

After a moment, Barry looked ahead. Dad had told him there would be a total of three traps. It had never occurred to him before what might happen if he failed. Would his father decide not to have *anyone* in the house hold the priesthood?

Holding the light purple thermos by his side, Barry walked deeper into the forest. They only owned fifteen acres, so he couldn't have much farther to go. After a few moments, he smelled the faintest whiff of smoke and headed for it.

Dad was waiting for him by a tiny campfire he seemed to have just started in a small clearing. The third trap must be face to face. Or perhaps Barry had missed the third trial altogether.

It didn't really matter, he realized, nodding to himself and walking calmly toward his father. Dad smiled and opened his arms, but his smile faded when he noticed the thermos in Barry's hand.

"Barry..." he whispered.

The two stood looking at each other in silence for a moment. Then Barry took another long sip from the thermos.

"It's Barbara," she replied.

A Plague on Both Your Cheeks

"I don't know how I can go on, Bishop," Duncan said.

Bishop Watson looked at him benevolently, his smile forcing wrinkles to appear alongside his lips and eyes. "Sandra's death is God's will," he said.

Duncan wrung his hands, staring at a paperweight on the bishop's desk. "But how can that be, Bishop? She was the only thing keeping me straight. Without her, I'm sure to have sex with a man."

Bishop Watson shook his head. "You will never be tempted above that which you are able," he said. "Heavenly Father has taken Sandra from you for a reason."

"Do I get to know what the reason is?"

Bishop Watson chuckled. "I had a dream last night while preparing for our interview today. I saw that Sandra was taken to the Other Side because she was needed there. Your wife was a successful young psychiatrist." The bishop paused, and Duncan wondered if the man was going to say something disparaging again about the poor choice Duncan had made in permitting his wife to work.

"Yes?" Duncan asked.

"Heavenly Father needed her in Spirit Prison to help all the spirits there who must deal with their porn addiction."

Duncan stared at the bishop. "Who's going to help *me* deal with my same-sex attraction?" Maybe Heavenly Father didn't love him enough to help. Maybe that was why he took Sandra away. At what point did he simply accept his fate and stop trying? He needed a sign. One way or the other, he needed a sign.

The bishop smiled widely, his smile lines etching more deeply into his face. "The Lord has blessed me with the solution to your problem."

"Really?" Then why in hell hadn't he told the Prophet?

"Rusty from the Elders Quorum has agreed to help. It will be part of his penance for smoking marijuana last month."

Duncan frowned. Rusty was a semi-active member with lots of tattoos and piercings. Those alone would probably keep him out of the Celestial Kingdom. He didn't know how anything Rusty could do would help him.

Maybe the Lord using such a sinner to bring about something good was a sign that Heavenly Father could still accomplish something worthwhile through Duncan, too.

"Rusty's going to inject a chip into your behind," the bishop went on. "It will be a tracking device. I'll be able to monitor you at any time, make sure you aren't heading to a gay bar or a porn store or some other ungodly place. If I see you in the wrong part of town, I'll give you a call on your cell. If I don't notice till after the fact, well, it'll still make your confession easier if I already know the truth."

Duncan's mouth fell open. On the one hand, he appreciated the bishop's efforts on his behalf. On the other…

"When can I see Rusty?"

Bishop Watson arranged for a meeting the following day after work. Rusty was an artist at a tattoo parlor in downtown Salt Lake, in an area the tracking device was sure to register as a problem if Duncan ever came back. He pulled off his pants and lay prone on a table.

It felt odd not wearing garments in front of another man. He could feel Rusty hovering over his ass and had the sudden thought that Rusty was a poor name for a tattoo artist. He felt something press against his left cheek and then felt a huge slap.

"What was that?" Duncan asked.

"I just implanted the chip," Rusty replied. Duncan started to move toward the edge of the table. "Oh, we're not done yet," Rusty continued.

"What do you mean?"

"Bishop Watson asked me to give you a small tattoo as well."

Weren't tattoos a sin? Wasn't that why Rusty smoked pot in the first place? But maybe the tattoo itself was a sign. A literal one.

"Don't worry. It's to keep you on the straight and narrow. And I'm good, so it won't hurt much."

Duncan failed to see how skill at tattooing could lessen the pain of three hundred needle strikes, but he didn't say anything. Whatever the design was, it covered both his cheeks. Duncan wondered if it was the bishop's telephone number. "If you can read this, please call…"

Too bad he'd already told the bishop he always fantasized about having someone do anal sex to him. It was worse than Winston accidentally divulging his fear of rats in *1984*. Duncan was willingly giving up all his secrets.

He just needed to know *one* of Heavenly Father's secrets.

"Keep that covered when you get home," Rusty told him when he finished. "It needs time to heal."

It wasn't until Sunday that Duncan was finally able to remove the bandages and look in the mirror. He stared in horror at what he saw. It wasn't only that "Jesus wept" was splayed in Gothic letters across his ass, but there were also two other tattoos. On his left cheek was a tattoo of a boil. On his right, a tattoo of a Kaposi's lesion.

Duncan's immediate thought was of Satan's plan in the Pre-Existence to come down to Earth and force everyone to obey the commandments. He caught the bishop in the hall after Sacrament meeting.

"I need to see you today," he said.

The bishop smiled and told him at what time to be in his office. Duncan had to wait two hours after all the meetings were over because Bishop Watson had other appointments already lined up, but he waited. As he sat on the sofa in the lobby, all he could feel was the pressure on his ass.

"What have you done to me, Bishop?" Duncan demanded the minute they were alone.

"I want to see you in the Celestial Kingdom one day," the bishop replied.

"But…but…my ass…"

"No one is ever going to see that except your next wife," Bishop Watson said. "Maybe a doctor, but he'll just get a kick out of it." He chuckled.

"I don't think I'm going to make it, Bishop," Duncan went on. "All I can think about now is my ass. I know I'm going to end up at a bar. And I won't bring my cell phone with me."

"No one you pick up at a bar will touch your behind."

"We'll have sex in the dark."

Bishop Watson tapped the triple combination sitting on his desktop. Then he tapped his priesthood manual. "I have a backup plan," he said.

"Yes?"

"How do you feel about your current job?"

Duncan worked at a hardware store. The bishop had suggested the job five years ago when he married Sandra, said it would expose him to true masculinity. Every two months, Duncan also had to report to the bishop's office to declare if Sandra was pregnant yet or not. Every two months, the answer was no.

It was hard to get your wife pregnant when she was wearing a strap-on and penetrating you every time you had sex.

Duncan had never been explicit enough to describe the sex he and his wife had practiced, and thankfully, Bishop Watson never pressed for details. Duncan knew the man suspected something, but he just kept encouraging Duncan to bring children into the world and give them bodies. Duncan kept saying he would.

"The job's okay."

Bishop Watson took a deep breath. "How would you feel about getting a job on an oil rig in the Gulf of Mexico?" he asked. "Or on a fishing boat in Alaska?"

"What?"

"A job like that will make a real man out of you."

Both jobs sounded awful, but then, they also sounded dangerous. If Duncan were killed at the age of thirty, that would mean forty-five years less temptation to face. Plus he'd get to see Sandra again. He did like Sandra, after all. Maybe a change in career was a sign.

"I like the cold more than I like the heat."

The bishop nodded. "Evil more than good. I understand. But maybe a few months in the cold will have you wanting to come back to the light and warmth of the gospel."

Duncan quit his job, stored some of his belongings at his parents' house in Orem, and then caught a plane to Anchorage. From there, he made his way to Dutch Harbor in Unalaska. And soon he was out to sea.

At first, the work was far too grueling to think about sex at all, even to remember the fact that he was trying to become straight. All he could think about was fish. They were after cod and threw out several ten-mile lines, with hooks every three feet, squid luring the fish to bite. It seemed that almost every day, Duncan suffered another cut or gash or bruise, but before long, he was working as if none of it mattered.

Because none of it did. Maybe his cuts would get infected. Perhaps he'd be thrown overboard in a swell. Maybe he'd get a concussion and then bleed out in his brain.

The bishop was right. Out here there was hope.

Duncan was working with Corbitt one day, pulling up a line of fish, when a huge black mound burst out of the sea.

"Goddamn orca," Corbitt mumbled. They saw orcas often. The whales heard the boat's hydraulics and knew by this point the sound meant fish. They'd pop up until they found a line and then scoop up half a mile or more, consuming everything the fishermen had caught.

Duncan looked at the creature, its mouth open, its teeth no more than three feet from his fingertips. It was a glorious sight. "But they're endangered, aren't they?" Duncan asked. It was probably good to feed them. If he wanted help, he had to be willing to offer it as well. Do unto others and all that. Maybe it was a sign.

"I'll go tell the captain to find another boat," Corbitt said. When orcas surfaced, the captain liked to navigate near other fishing boats, hoping the whales would be distracted and latch onto someone else's lines.

Corbitt's departure gave Duncan a few moments to relax. There was something to be said, he thought, for not having the time to think about sin. He'd been propositioned a few times, of course. An all-male crew needed to find sexual release somehow. There was only one room full of hammocks for the sleeping arrangements, but there weren't enough spots for the entire crew.

They slept in shifts, and since the men only had a chance to shower once a week, both the men and the hammocks and pretty much everything else on board always smelled like fish.

How could Duncan even consider having sex when all he could smell was fish?

"If you don't want to smell my dick," Corbitt had told him, "you can always just let me fuck you."

Duncan glared out at the orca. Damn that whale for giving him time to think.

The captain changed course, the orcas drifted off, and Corbitt slapped Duncan on the ass. They began collecting fish again. As the day wore on, the seas grew rougher, and they had to stop fishing. Inside, Duncan looked out the window, and when the boat rose up high on a wave, the window was facing straight down. Corbitt was behind him, pressing him against the glass.

"Ten fish," Corbitt noted. He pointed to the line of fish dangling from the side of the boat, hooked cod three feet apart from the deck all the way to the bottom of the swell. "A thirty-foot wave."

"Are we gonna die?" Duncan asked. Perhaps the storm was a sign. Maybe everything was finally over. Please, Heavenly Father, please.

Corbitt laughed. "It'll get worse before it gets better."

Just like life, Duncan thought. But things *would* finally get better. He'd become straight. Or at least straighter. He'd get married to a woman in the temple again. He'd have sex where he did the penetrating.

"You know what makes afternoons like this better?" Corbitt reached around Duncan's waist for his belt buckle.

"Corbitt…"

"It'll be fine. Everybody does it. We'd go crazy otherwise." Corbitt finished unbuckling Duncan's belt and pulled his pants and bottom garments down. There were other crewmembers nearby, but no one said a word.

Except Corbitt. "What the—"

Duncan wasn't going to say anything. Corbitt would be repulsed and walk away. The bishop's plan was working. Duncan's virtue was saved. It was a sign that everything was going to be all right.

"You are one freaky fuck." Corbitt laughed. He dabbed something on Duncan's asshole and then pressed his dick against it. The boat lifted. "Hold on," said Corbitt, "this is the best way to do it." When the boat slammed back down, the man's penis thrust deeply inside Duncan's ass from the blow. Duncan groaned.

It hadn't worked, Duncan thought in confusion. This wasn't supposed to happen. The bishop must not have been inspired, after all.

But how could that be? The tracking device would show that Duncan was nowhere near a gay bar. There'd be no alert. No way to receive a cell phone call if there were.

Blood swirled and roiled inside his head, and it wasn't from the storm. He had suffered the pain of the tattoos, had quit his job, had endured miserable work conditions and rips in his skin and the nauseating smell of fish day after day after day. And he was still going to Hell.

There were another two weeks left before they headed back to Dutch Harbor. Corbitt's stabbing penetration was a sign.

"That wasn't so bad, was it?" Corbitt asked, pulling out.

Maybe Duncan could keep working on the boat for another six months, or a year, or two years. Sooner or later, he'd certainly be killed on the job. And maybe Sandra could then help him in Spirit Prison to overcome his same-sex attraction. She'd been doing such a good job before she died accidentally from a prescription overdose.

If there was porn in Spirit Prison, there must be strap-ons. He missed Sandra.

"Go get someone else," Duncan said.

"Huh?"

"I'm open for business now. May as well get a Magic Marker and write it on here." He patted his ass. "See if anyone else needs to relax during the storm."

Corbitt laughed. "You're finally fish-broken," he said. "We all give in to guy sex sooner or later. But you don't have to go overboard."

"Go get Andy." Duncan pointed to another of the crew members he'd always thought was kind of cute, in a *Walking Dead* sort of way.

Corbitt laughed again and made his way over to their crewmate, telling him something that put a smile on Andy's face. Andy came over and hung on to Duncan as the ship rolled. Duncan felt the pain of having his sphincter opened too quickly again and groaned. He looked out the window and counted eleven fish.

Smoking Beer and Drinking Marijuana

"Hatch!" Elliott shouted into the phone. "Oh, my God! Hatch!"

"What's wrong, Elliott?" What could it be now, Hatch wondered, turning the radio down. With Elliott, it was always something.

"Our house burned down! Dad fell asleep with a cigarette. We've lost everything!"

Hatch felt a part of his heart close off. He'd known Elliott for over two years, and the man suffered one disaster after another after another. The only thing in common among all the catastrophes was that Hatch ended up losing money. "Is anyone hurt?" he asked.

"No, no. We got out of the house all right. But we didn't have time to take anything with us." Elliott was panting, as if he'd run a mile to the nearest phone. But Hatch had bought him a cell phone a year ago and had been paying the bill ever since.

"Where are you staying tonight?"

"With my cousin Jill and her boyfriend. But we can't stay there long. That's why I'm calling."

Of course it was.

"My dad and I are going to need to find a new apartment. We'll need help with the deposit and the first month's rent."

"I see."

"And maybe with getting some new furniture."

"One thing at a time, Elliott."

"Sure, Hatch. Sure."

Hatch thought for a moment. He'd already bought Elliott a small used car and was helping him make the payments every month. He'd already paid for the training program Elliott wanted so he could start working on tugboats in the Mississippi River. And he paid Elliott a hundred dollars every time the man let Hatch give him a hand job. Hatch didn't have a lot left over.

"Can you come over around noon tomorrow?" Hatch asked. "I'll have some money for you then."

"Oh, you're so wonderful, Hatch!"

Uh-huh.

Hatch hung up the phone and walked slowly to his computer, where he logged onto his account at Crescent City Credit Union. He transferred $1200 from his savings to his checking and then logged off with a scowl at the monitor. He couldn't begin to add up the thousands he'd spent on the young man. He'd first met him by answering an ad in the local New Orleans gay paper.

But Elliott didn't really want to be a prostitute for the rest of his life. He had ambition. That was one of the things which attracted Hatch to him. Hatch paid for a couple of semesters at Delgado Community College, helped here and there with rent and groceries, and helped him with doctor bills. The young man always seemed to be sick.

Hatch punched the numbers on his cell for his friend JW. Hatch always joked that JW was an ex-Jehovah's Witness like Hatch was an ex-Mormon. Of course, in reality JW was a lapsed Catholic, the most common condition for a New Orleanian. "Hi, Hatch!" JW said cheerily as he answered the phone. "Are we still on for tonight?"

"Yes. I just wanted to confirm. 7:00 at the Orpheum?"

"Sounds great. Then a drink at Pocket Pool? Tonight is New Meat Night."

"I can't wait. See you at 7:00." Hatch hung up. He knew the call had been completely unnecessary. The plans had already been made, and JW never bailed on him. Why was it so hard for young people to be reliable? Was it just a matter of the era in which they'd been raised?

JW was seventy-seven, a year younger than Hatch. Elliott was a mere twenty-seven. Somehow, during all the time Hatch spent with the young man, he'd gotten involved with his father as well. Murphy was fifty-three, an alcoholic who barely made enough money to pay for his booze, much less the rent. But he was a genuinely nice guy.

Hatch couldn't help but like him. He made drawings of Elliott, portraits mostly but also scenes of Elliott eating dinner or watching TV or even that great drawing of Elliott getting out of the shower. And Murphy gave them all to Hatch to repay him for helping so often with the bills.

Which made Murphy a very well-paid artist.

A well-paid ex-con artist. Both Murphy and Elliott had been in jail more than a few times, mostly for bad checks and public drunkenness but also for one father/son burglary. Elliott never wanted to talk about it much and said he was a new man since he'd met Hatch.

He took the training program Hatch paid for and started working on a tugboat in the River, but of course, one illness after another kept him away from the job so much he ended up being demoted after a few months. At least he hadn't been fired, though. Elliott did earn a *little* money on his own. But he'd sworn off prostitution, except for Hatch, so he didn't make much.

"I'm not really gay," Elliott had told him on their second date. "I'm really only comfortable getting a hand job or a blow job." Hatch had seen a discharge the moment Elliott had stripped that evening, so hand job it was, and hand job it had been ever since.

Hatch and JW enjoyed the symphony that evening, a night of Tchaikovsky. Then they headed a few blocks into the Quarter, where Hatch was lucky enough to find parking within fifty feet of Pocket Pool. It took JW a little longer to find a spot. Hatch bought a Grasshopper and nursed it for the next ninety minutes as he and JW watched the dancers flex and gyrate on top of the bar.

Of the six young men, only two were worth tipping. Hatch always brought enough ones to be able to tip throughout the evening. Tonight, JW also liked one of the men Hatch liked, so they kept trying to out-tip each other.

Thinking about all the money he was going to lose the following day, Hatch let JW win.

Finally, it was time to go. "Thanks for going out with me this evening, Hatch. You're always a fun time."

"You are, too." If only the man were fifty years younger, sixty pounds lighter, and two inches longer. They'd never had sex, but they'd both gone to pee in the bar bathroom together at the same time, so Hatch knew what he was working with. He hated being so superficial but looks mattered to him.

He'd been with George almost thirty years before his partner died of pancreatic cancer, and George had never been much of a looker. Hatch had frequently felt embarrassed when out with him in public. But he did love him. The cancer had given the man a long, grueling death, something Hatch never wanted to experience again.

So in the seventeen years that followed, he never even considered dating anyone romantically. He had friends, of course, and he had his hustlers and escorts, but there were no boyfriends.

Hatch thought about his days as a Mormon missionary in Norway back in the late 1950's. Members had taken him in and loved him. He'd fallen in love with one of his companions, too. But the moment Hatch told his fellow missionary how he felt, he'd been shipped home, excommunicated, and cut off from the friends and family he'd known for years.

It was why he could never quite sever ties with Elliott. The guy was a lemon if ever there was one. It probably wasn't even the young man's fault. Or at least not completely. But fault or blame weren't the issues. The fact was that this young fellow was always going to be trouble. Hatch could see it clearly, but it would be cruel to stop meeting with him.

As soon as he was back in his Marigny condo, he called Elliott on his cell. "My juice is about to run out," Elliott said. "I'll need to buy a new charger."

"I just wanted to hear your voice again. I thought about you all night."

"You're so sweet, Hatch. I'll see you tomorrow at noon."

* * *

"Hatch! Oh, my God! Hatch!"

"What is it, Elliott? What's happened?" He turned the radio down.

"My dad just died! What am I going to do?"

"It's going to be okay, Elliott. Don't worry. It's going to be okay."

Hatch had been expecting this for a few months. Ever since the fire, Murphy had been drinking more heavily. His liver was taxed, and he suffered two medium sized heart attacks. It had been Hatch who always came through with the money for this test or that prescription or this other procedure.

And it wasn't as if Murphy was the only one with medical bills. Elliott cut his hand while working on his car.

The cut became infected, and Elliott almost lost his hand. Since the injury wasn't work related, the tugboat company wouldn't pay for it. While Elliott had insurance from work, it wasn't enough to pay for everything.

Hatch spent thousands and thousands on both the young man and his father. He'd thought he had enough money in savings to last if he lived to ninety, but now he wasn't sure he'd have enough to make it to eighty.

"What am I going to do?"

"Your father wasn't helping with the rent in any event," Hatch said soothingly. "And I'm still here to help with that. You're going to stay in your apartment and you're going to keep going to work, and everything is going to be fine."

Elliott sniffed on the other end of the line. "You really think so?"

"Yes, I do."

"Can I come over tonight?" Elliott asked. "I think I need to feel good for a bit."

Hatch knew he didn't mean he wanted to be hugged. "Sure," he said.

"The car's still not running. Will you pay for a cab?"

Hatch sighed. "Sure."

"See you in thirty minutes."

Hatch punched in JW's number and waited for his friend to answer. "Hey, Hatch. We still on for the movie tonight at the Broad theater?"

"I'm afraid not."

"Elliott again?"

"I'll make it up to you, JW. Are you up for a movie tomorrow night?"

There was a pause on the line. "I don't think so," JW said finally.

After they hung up, Hatch paced back and forth across his condo. He hardly noticed the paintings and sculptures he'd bought over the years, one of the pleasures of retiring with money. He hadn't been able to go to a gallery in almost two years. There'd be no point. He'd even had to sell one of his paintings to JW, but that exchange seemed to hurt their relationship more than solidify it.

Hatch was being a Good Samaritan. Why wasn't he being blessed for it? Life only seemed to grow worse and worse. He was going to the chiropractor more, his back muscles constantly in knots. He hardly ever had energy for the gym these days, and he'd always loved working out, looking at the hunks all around him. Here he was, seventy-nine years old, and still a trim hundred and sixty pounds.

He wasn't sure how old his parents had lived to be, hadn't spoken to them in decades, but he remembered his grandparents back in the day being healthy into their old age. He thought he probably had good genes. He wanted to live to a hundred. But soon he'd have to start selling off more of his artwork. His savings were almost depleted.

A short while later, the doorbell rang. Hatch grabbed his wallet and opened the door. Elliott held out his hand. "It's twenty dollars," he said. Hatch handed him a bill. He came back a moment later and gave Hatch a tight hug. "You're so good to me," he said. "I don't know what I'd do without you. You love me even more than my father ever did."

"Oh, I know he loved you, too."

"But not as much as you. Come on, let's go upstairs."

Hatch had put aside an extra hundred for the evening.

* * *

Hatch picked up his phone. "Elliott?" he asked. No one spoke on the other end. Perhaps Elliott had simply butt-called him. He was about to hang up when he heard a loud sniff. "Elliott?" he asked. He turned down the radio. "Are you okay?"

"The doctor said I have six months to live!" he sobbed.

Hatch lowered the phone and took a deep breath. He'd suspected something like this was coming. After Elliott had been brutally mugged and then a few days later developed pneumonia, the doctor had said the young man's lung capacity was permanently damaged.

After that, a bout of Hepatitis C had done damage to his liver. God only knew what had caused the impairment to his kidneys. Hatch felt his heart leap, not in anguish but in joy. Soon this horrible ordeal might finally be over.

He bit his lip so hard it almost bled. What kind of monster would think such a thing?

But if he handled this right, Hatch could still make his trip to Atlanta this weekend. The dancers there were so much more attractive than the ones in New Orleans. JW was originally going to make the trip with him, but they'd had a falling out two weeks ago, and his friend had canceled.

"It's going to be okay," Hatch said soothingly. "You'll still be able to live on your own for a good while yet. Nothing has to be decided today."

"I got mad and threw a beer bottle through my window," said Elliott. "The landlord is kicking me out."

Hatch felt a flush of anger. Life was hard enough without people making it even worse than it had to be. He did *not* want to live with anyone again. He did *not* want to take care of a dying man again. He wanted to be free.

"Have you been drinking marijuana again?" Hatch asked. It was a private joke between the two of them. When Hatch had been a boy, he was so ignorant of anything outside Mormonism that he'd once told his mother, "I heard that Brother Anderson smokes beer." His mother hadn't even corrected him.

When he told Elliott, the young man laughed and laughed. At first, it had felt like a shared laughter, but after it went on a bit too long, Hatch began to feel that Elliott was laughing at him, not with him. But he still couldn't help bringing it up any time things grew too tense.

Hatch wanted to laugh again, feel light and happy. Thinking about his Mormon childhood didn't really accomplish that, of course. Instead, he felt a deep longing for those old times when everyone was kind and good and gentle.

"You can't come here," Hatch said firmly. His lab tests were all out of whack these past few months. The stress was killing him. If he took Elliott in, he'd end up dying even before Elliott did. No. He couldn't do it. It might be selfish and mean, but he had to be strong.

He only had five pieces of artwork left, in a condo that had once been filled to capacity with great paintings and sculptures. Soon the only thing left would be the drawings of Elliott. He was down to $9000 in the bank. He still had his pension, but that would only serve him if Elliott was no longer around to keep bleeding him dry.

Perhaps the young man would only live five months, thought Hatch. Maybe only four. "I'll find you a room to rent," he said.

"A room?"

"Do you need a mansion?"

"No, no, I guess not."

"I'll make some calls, find a place, and then I'll come pick you up and help you pack a few things."

"I have to leave behind all this nice furniture you got me?"

"It was all from Goodwill. It'll be okay." He pulled the phone away so Elliott wouldn't hear him grind his teeth. Then he brought the phone back to his face. "I'll be over in about two hours."

"Okay, Hatch. Okay. But then can you jack me off again? You always make me feel better."

Elliott still charged him, even after all the rest.

Hatch hadn't thought about religion in years, other than to spit at the television every time some Republican politician said something repulsive. But Elliott would be going over to the Other Side soon. If there was such a thing. And unless Elliott died soon, Hatch would be there before long as well. Would he see George again? Would he see his parents? Would his parents even want to see him?

He hated that Elliott was making him worry about such things.

Hatch didn't want to die. He wanted to go see the new Spielberg movie. He wanted to go to the opera. He wanted to go to Pocket Pool. He wanted to go to Atlanta.

Why had he ever answered that damn ad in the newspaper? It was like having sex without a condom. One moment of pleasure followed by years of misery.

But he did love Elliott. At home with so much time recovering, the young man had started taking up drawing himself. He wasn't as good as his father, and his injured hand hadn't helped matters any, but he drew self-portraits of himself in the mirror, or looking down at his penis.

There were lots of drawings of his penis. He even drew his hand holding it sometimes, and the hand looked real. Hatch had heard that faces and hands were the hardest parts for an artist to get right.

The young man was sweet and beautiful and talented.

And the worst thing that had ever happened to Hatch.

Hatch had retired from Mormonism at the age of twenty. He'd retired from marriage at the age of sixty. And from teaching at the age of sixty-six. More than anything he wanted to retire from Elliott. Maybe after recuperating for a year or two, he'd rally and still manage to enjoy another ten or fifteen.

There was clearly no god to protect him. So it *must* be okay to look out for himself. There was nothing wrong with self-preservation.

He wanted to be free!

Hatch browsed the Internet, made some phone calls, and found a room to rent only a mile away. Paying for that would be a lot cheaper than the rent he had to keep coughing up for Elliott now. Maybe things would start getting better even before the young man died. He climbed into his Jeep Cherokee and drove across the River to Elliott's apartment in Westwego. Elliott was waiting at the door.

"I've packed my best clothes," he said, "and my sketchpad and pencils." He forced a smile. "I'm ready."

They drove in silence. Hatch didn't want to hear happy songs on the radio. Or sad ones, either, for that matter.

"We're going to stop at your condo first, aren't we?" asked Elliott. "We have time for a hand job before we go to my new place, don't we? At least then I'll have some spending money."

"I'll help you with your things," Hatch said as they pulled into his parking space, the iron gate closing behind them. He smiled but Elliott now looked confused. "It's okay," he said. "I've made some room for you in my closet."

Elliott's look of confusion slowly turned into a beautiful smile, that same smile which always melted Hatch's heart. "Come on inside."

"I love you, Hatch."

Hatch nodded and opened the door.

Suicide Center #212

"You're up again, Albert," said Gretchen, pointing to the computer screen. "Room 9."

Albert nodded and headed down the hall to meet the next patient. It was 4:30, almost the end of the workday, but Albert wasn't looking forward to going home. In some ways, he was jealous of all the people who were choosing suicide. It would be so great to finally be done with it all. But as a born-again Christian, he knew that suicide was a sin. These were all people going to hell, anyway, but at least they were able to escape the misery of life.

Albert walked through the door with a smile and nodded to the young, dark-haired man sitting on the examining table. He had a day's growth of beard. What poor self-control not to groom oneself for a moment like this.

"Good morning," Albert said. "It's a great day to die."

He was supposed to say this to every new patient here at the Suicide Center in north Seattle. Similar centers were located throughout the country. The young man smiled weakly in return, showing a dimple on the left side of his face. Asymmetrical. He didn't particularly look Muslim or Jewish, but it was practically impossible to tell who the atheists were. The gays were a little easier to spot, but Albert was often surprised to discover a perfectly normal looking man was gay.

Thank goodness he'd never told anyone about his own homosexuality. He'd suppressed those base desires and married a lovely woman ten years ago when he was twenty-five. They now had three children, all being raised as true Christians. It was a great society the new president was creating, where fewer people would even be tempted to do bad things anymore.

"Can we get this over with?" asked the young man. He rubbed his forehead with the back of his hand. Albert noted the firm muscles of his arm. Small muscles, to be sure, but still hard. Albert shivered a little.

"Geoff," said Albert, reading off the computer screen, "we just need you to sign a few papers transferring ownership of any and all properties over to the state, and we can move ahead."

"It's not going to hurt, is it?" The young man's brows furrowed.

Albert laughed as he'd been trained to do in response to this question. "You'll drink a warm cup of a sweet liquid, you'll fall asleep, and you'll never wake up." Well, that was the way it used to be done, anyway, before the cost of the medication became too prohibitive and they switched to their current method.

"Chad went to the camps," said Geoff, looking at the floor. "He didn't want to die with me."

"And who's Chad?" Albert asked casually, trying to keep the conversation calm and easy. He placed some papers in front of Geoff and handed him a pen. He pointed to the signature lines. Geoff scribbled his name.

"Chad was my boyfriend. I thought we were going to be married. I thought we were going to have a life together. But then…"

Yes, then. The world had changed almost overnight when the new administration took office. Registries, closed borders, deportations, suppression of the press. It was impossible to list all the changes. As promised, the new president and Congress brought manufacturing back to the U.S., but that didn't create the jobs he'd guaranteed, because all the new factories were inside internment camps.

People on "the list" could choose either to go to a suicide center or to a camp. In the camps, they'd make phones or televisions or radios or clothing or whatever, in exchange for the opportunity to continue living in this great nation. They had, of course, also been required to sign everything over to the government when they were given their prisoner numbers, and they didn't receive a penny for their labors.

"Everyone knows gay love isn't the same as real love," Albert said soothingly. "I know it's a hard thing to accept, but Chad proved it, didn't he? It's healthier to face facts. Makes life easier."

"Life," Geoff muttered. "Chad said we'd only have to endure the camps for a few years, and then it would all be over, just like the Holocaust finally came to an end."

Albert laughed. "Apples and oranges, don't you think?" He put the signed papers away. "Just like gay love and real love."

"I really loved *him*," said Geoff.

"I know it feels that way. Really, I do. Now, we're going to get you set up for your drink. No more suffering. You'll go to sleep and rest peacefully forever."

"No, I won't," Geoff replied. "I'll go to Spirit Prison. That's where bad Mormons go. And I'm a bad Mormon. My parents were the ones who talked me into coming here. They said it would show Heavenly Father I was repentant."

Albert looked at the young man and shuddered. This was his first Mormon. A Mormon like Albert had been before meeting Miriam. Well, not exactly like Albert. Albert had stayed pure. He may well have given up exaltation by choosing Miriam, but he'd at least ensured his salvation. She was the only woman who ever expressed even a minimal interest in him. He was left with choosing between being true to the Church or obeying the commandment to be heterosexual.

"And *are* you repentant?" he asked. If the young man could stop being gay, he wouldn't have to die. Of course, Albert knew that he himself was still gay, and that was after a full decade of a normal marriage. What hope was there for a young man who'd already been practicing the sins of the flesh?

It was sad. So, so sad. The young man was quite attractive. His firm thighs strained against his slacks. Such a loss. If only he could marry Miriam, too.

Albert had often fantasized about polyandry. Joseph Smith had practiced it, hadn't he? But Miriam only said insulting things about the man. She even sometimes hinted that she didn't think Albert was a real Christian because of his heretical background.

She liked to sing "Amazing Grace" while they had sex. He got erections now whenever he opened a hymnbook.

There was a tap on the door, and Gretchen poked her head into the room. "Albert, the truck's getting ready to go." She nodded toward Geoff.

"Thank you, Gretchen." The lifeless bodies were shipped to the camps to provide protein for the workers. After processing by inmates in other designated internment centers, of course. You couldn't let people know they were eating other people. The general public couldn't know these things, either.

There was no success without manipulation. Albert needed to hurry this up. There was always a push to get just one more body on the truck. Maybe two. He didn't know why he was taking so long. Usually, the whole thing was done within two minutes.

"Take off your shoes," Albert instructed. The young man did so. "And take off your shirt."

"My shirt?"

That part was solely for Albert's benefit. He knew he'd pay for it on Judgment Day, but with some of these young men, he simply couldn't resist. "We want you to be as comfortable as possible." He watched Geoff remove his shirt, and he felt a stirring in his groin.

If only he could come here as a patient himself. All the unhappiness would finally be over.

Was it a sin to be jealous of a man about to die?

"Now I'm going to recline the table a bit," Albert said. "Let me strap you in so you don't fall off." He reached over and tightened Velcro belts across Geoff's chest and waist. He could feel the warmth emanating from the man's body. He looked at Geoff's nipples and wanted so desperately to touch one.

"You have to pin my arms down, too?" asked Geoff.

"The straps create a sensation of being hugged," Albert replied. "We find that it helps."

"I wish…I wish…" The young man looked forlorn.

"How did you meet Chad?" asked Albert. He didn't know why he said such a thing.

"It was a couple of years after my mission to Chile," Geoff replied.

Albert had served on the other side of the Andes in Paraguay. He was tempted to say something in Spanish but resisted. The man could know nothing about him. He wanted to sing a Sacrament hymn. He wanted to sing a Primary song. He wanted to quote his favorite Book of Mormon scripture: There must needs be opposition in all things.

He wanted to wear garments again with this man.

"I was still living at home and attending the University of Washington," Geoff continued, "still dependent on my parents. So when I knew I had to accept my orientation and leave the Church, I needed help."

"Yes?"

"Chad was part of the Underground Handcart Company. It was a group of ex-Mormons who helped young people find the funds and support they needed to break away."

There'd been nothing to help Albert. He'd put up with all the condemnation from his family because he knew that if *they* knew the reason he'd become born again, they'd have agreed it was the lesser of two evils. As a Christian, he could always be baptized into the Church again when he was an old man. But he'd never be able to undo a life of degeneracy.

Albert started to reach for Geoff's hair but then stopped himself. He wished they gave injections so he could look at the man's butt. He wished he had to take an anal temperature reading. "So he took advantage of you when you were vulnerable," he said.

Geoff shook his head. "It wasn't like that. Chad…Chad loved me."

"And he's letting you die alone without him."

"I can't blame him for wanting to live. It's what normal people do. He's a fighter." He sighed. "Not like me."

Albert wanted to abandon his wife and children and go to heaven right now. Even to a lower degree. He'd give anything to be able to die without it being a sin. Back before the Purge, he'd gone to Pioneer Square at midnight to hand out money to the homeless, hoping to be killed in a mugging.

He'd asked for drugs with the longest list of side effects to treat his depression. He'd even gone on long hikes praying to get lost in the woods. He couldn't deliberately leave the trail, of course. That would be suicide. But he could hope to get turned around accidentally.

It never happened, though. He had a natural map inside his brain. He always knew his location.

And Miriam and the kids were always waiting for him when he returned.

"What's the point of living?" Albert asked. "If you know you're damned anyway. You may as well have everything settled."

Geoff looked up at him with pain in his eyes. "Do you really think I'm damned?"

"I'm—I'm just repeating what you said. Spirit Prison or whatever."

"Yes," said Geoff sadly. "Spirit Prison."

Could there really be internment camps in heaven? Surely, there had to be peace for everyone at some point. If one didn't make it to heaven with God, that loving God couldn't send people to burn for eternity, could he? He'd never believed Miriam's preacher on that point.

But Outer Darkness seemed equally as bad. Surely, an all-powerful God could just make people disappear forever. Snap his fingers. Wave a scepter. There had to be spiritual death, too. Anything else would simply be too mean. And God wasn't supposed to be mean.

He'd allowed all the homeless to be rounded up and executed, hadn't he?

There was another tap at the door. "The truck's waiting," Gretchen said through the crack. Her tone indicated irritation.

"I'll be out in a minute," Albert replied, a bit tartly. Damn those stretch goals. Gretchen frowned and closed the door.

"What's the medicine taste like?" asked Geoff.

"We have different flavors. Almond, blackberry, and pineapple. Hot chocolate is our most popular." Could you go to hell for lying, even if the lie was to make someone's death easier?

"I think I'll take the almond."

"Almond it is. Now close your eyes and relax. Here's a shade to put over your eyes." He slipped the eye cover onto Geoff's head.

"I have to drink with my eyes closed?"

"It's best this way. More soothing. I'll give you a straw, and I'll hold it for you since your arms are strapped down." Albert pushed a button, and a soft Chopin melody filled the air. He opened a drawer and pulled out a roll of plastic wrap. A couple of quick passes over the patient's head and he'd suffocate within two minutes. It was completely painless, though undoubtedly frightening. People always struggled, even when they said they wanted to die.

Why couldn't they afford the necessary medication, Albert wondered, if they were confiscating everyone's property? Surely, there was enough money, even with the millions of doses they needed.

Albert stood over the reclined examining table, frowning. How could Chad have possibly given up this beautiful man? Perhaps it wasn't Chad but Geoff who was a prick, he thought with sudden understanding. Maybe he said mean things. Maybe he didn't keep the house clean.

What Albert wouldn't give to live in a dirty house with a man like Geoff.

God, you're killing me, Albert thought, looking up at the ceiling in despair.

If only God really would kill him.

Who could possibly choose the misery of an internment camp over the bliss of death? Who could choose a lonely eternity over the damnation of love?

"Put your shirt back on." Albert reached over and unfastened the straps across Geoff's body.

"What's going on?"

"We're getting out of here."

"I...don't understand." Geoff buttoned his shirt and began pulling on his shoes.

"We'll have to sneak out the side entrance. Our only hope is to get across the mountains before they catch us. Then we can head north through the desert. We'll probably have to go on foot. Get off the main roads. Get off even the smaller roads."

"Go to Canada?" Geoff breathed in astonishment. "What about the drones?"

"It's a long shot, but I keep a few jugs of water in my trunk at all times, and…" He'd studied maps of the area just in case this day ever came. There were rumors of an Underground Airport, though he had no idea how to contact them.

It was hard to get real news to verify anything, but they might get away. They might. Geoff would be so grateful that he'd choose to stay with Albert. They'd have a life together somewhere else. The beautiful young man would forget about Chad.

If they were lucky, they'd be killed before they reached the border.

Albert cracked the door to the examining room open and peered down the hall. Then he turned back to Geoff and put a finger to his lips. He held out his hand and motioned for the other man to follow.

Lending a Hand…and Other Body Parts

"You're creeping me out, David." Gareth shifted farther away from me on the sofa.

"But don't you feel sorry for them?" I asked. "They never get to taste cheesecake. Never get to feel a cool breeze on their skin on a hot day." Never get to have sex, I wanted to add, though that was sometimes true even for people who did have bodies.

"I might have felt sorry for someone like an individual Japanese soldier during World War II, but that doesn't mean it would have been a good idea to invite him over for dinner."

"And why not? If you take away his gun first and don't let him contact the rest of his troop, what harm could there be?"

Gareth sighed. "Don't you see, David? That's exactly the problem. I mean, I don't believe you can really be possessed by a spirit in the first place, despite all those stories we heard as missionaries. But if you can be, how are you going to keep this guy from contacting his friends? How are you going to make sure he has no power? He'll probably end up having *more* power once he's no longer a disembodied spirit." He blinked. "Sheesh."

I shrugged. "I guess so. It just seems unnecessarily cruel that so many billions of my brothers and sisters will never get to have a body of their own, just because they followed Lucifer in the Pre-Existence."

"You're second-guessing God now?" Gareth shook his head. "You may end up in Outer Darkness one day with all those evil spirits anyway. Let one into your body then." He closed his eyes. "What a ridiculous conversation to be having. It's crazy talk. You sound like Sister Myers who's always going on about her cat during Fast and Testimony meeting."

"Okay, okay," I said. "I'll read an extra chapter from the Book of Mormon tonight to get back on track."

"You should probably read two extra chapters." He stood up and offered his hand. "I'd better get going."

I reached for his hand but then pulled him over against me and gave him a hug. "You're a good friend, Gareth."

Gareth pulled away and frowned. "I'm not sure we should be hugging yet." He shook my hand firmly.

"See you at church on Sunday," I said. Gareth gave my shoulder a tap and walked out of the apartment. After I locked the door behind him, I sat back down on my sofa. Gareth and I had been friends since before our missions. We'd become Eagle Scouts together back when that was a thing. We'd both served two years in Europe, me in Finland and he in Belgium. We'd even toured the rest of Europe together before we came home, against the wishes of our respective mission presidents.

And we were both studying Biology now at the University of Utah, in our senior year. We quizzed each other on molecular pathways for Biochemistry. We sat next to each other in Institute. We were Home Teaching companions.

I thought he would understand.

For years, I'd reflected on the state of those who'd been cast out of heaven. They hadn't killed anyone. They hadn't had sex outside of marriage. All they'd done was pick the wrong Plan of Salvation. It didn't seem so grievous a sin that they should be denied the opportunity to repent. If we could just show them a little kindness, treat them like real, three-dimensional people, their hearts might be softened and we could welcome them back into the fold.

Since missionary work here on Earth wasn't going very well these days, why not try to persuade some spirits? That's what temple work was all about, after all. The only difference was which pool of spirits we were drawing from.

I went to my bedroom and picked up my triple combination. But instead of reading from the Book of Mormon, I read the entire Book of Abraham. When I finished, I knelt beside my bed and prayed, knowing I'd receive an answer. I'd followed the correct procedure for making decisions. I'd studied the issue and come to a conclusion. Now I just needed the confirmation of the Holy Ghost.

I felt a little tingle, but not the overwhelming flush I was hoping for. Yet I also didn't experience the stupor of thought that would have told me no. Perhaps all it meant was that although Heavenly Father wasn't overly thrilled with my plan, he wasn't 100% against it, either.

After I finished praying, I cleared my throat and began to speak. We'd been taught that Satan and his followers couldn't read minds, so I had to do this out loud. "Hey," I said, looking about the room, "one of you guys without a body."

I had a sudden flashback to a scene in *Ghost* where evil spirits surround one of the characters, and I started to feel a little creeped out myself. "Hey," I said again, "I'm okay with just *one* of you coming into my body for a few days." I held up a warning hand. "It has to be a male spirit, though. I don't want any weird sexual conflicts inside me."

Now I held out both hands in supplication. "But one of you can come in, see how much better our Plan of Salvation is that allows you to have a body, and maybe change allegiance. I'm offering myself up to you. Consider it an olive branch." I continued looking about the room. I saw nothing out of the ordinary, though. No moving shadows. No shimmer in the air. No wind rustling the blinds.

But maybe Satan simply wouldn't let any of his followers leave, like Communists building the Berlin Wall. He did seem to be a control freak, after all. That had been the whole point of his plan in the first place.

I brushed my teeth, read two chapters from the Book of Mormon, and went to bed. In some ways, I thought, being asleep was a little like being a spirit. You could fly. You could be in one place one minute and in another place the next. You couldn't feel anything if you tried to pinch yourself. You were just your mind.

Maybe that was better than being confined to a mortal container with limited abilities. But then, it was the nature of some of those abilities which made the difference.

Sometime during the night, probably in my third REM cycle, I had a dream that a spirit with no physical form had slipped into my body. I seemed to actually *feel* it, the way you could feel the sun coming out or going behind a cloud while you were lying outside on a blanket with your eyes closed. And I could sense that this being was overjoyed at the opportunity to be encased in flesh. He wanted to hug me in gratitude but couldn't.

I woke up to discover I was masturbating under the sheets.

"Stop that!" I commanded.

"You didn't honestly think this wouldn't be the first thing I tried, did you?" The voice echoed inside my head. But it didn't sound like my own internal thought. I could *hear* that someone else was speaking.

"Oh, my heck!" I breathed.

"Stop distracting me and let me finish."

I admit I was a little irked. The main point of my invitation was to try to help this guy repent, and here he was committing a serious sin the moment he had the chance. Of course, in the big scheme of things, I didn't suppose it was all *that* serious. I confessed it to my bishop too often myself and hadn't been disfellowshipped or anything. Besides, I got to feel the orgasm this time without being personally responsible for it. I wouldn't need to confess a thing.

This might work out.

"Oh, man, that felt good. Thanks a lot." He reached down beside the bed and had me pick up a hand towel I'd left there for situations like this. How embarrassing that he knew it was there. He must have been watching me on other nights. Thank goodness he'd only been able to see me on those occasions and not read my thoughts at the time. There were differing levels of mortification.

"Can I ask your name?" Since he was inside my head, we seemed perfectly able to communicate by thoughts now. Though I hadn't been able to detect what he'd been fantasizing about a few minutes earlier. I wasn't sure I wanted to know. He might have been fantasizing about my mother, after all, or the bishop's wife.

"I'm Ebenezer."

"I'm David."

"Nice to meet you." He chuckled and cupped my balls. "You have a nice penis."

I was a little taken aback. It hardly seemed like something a person you'd just met would say. "Uh, thank you." This must be how a conjoined twin felt any time he tried to do something private.

"Do you have any ice cream in the freezer? I've been dying to try it out."

I got up and plodded my way to the kitchen. Even though Ebenezer seemed to be letting me navigate, his presence was partly in control, too. I ran into the wall once and then bumped against the side of the counter. But I eventually plopped a single scoop of vanilla ice cream into a bowl and let my new companion grab a spoon.

"Oh, this is good! I want to try chocolate tomorrow. And then strawberry. And then butter pecan, and then—"

"I'm not letting you make me fat," I said.

There was a moment of silence, and I wondered if I'd offended him. Then I heard the sound of his voice again. "You're right. Let's go look in the mirror." He moved my right leg, and we again stumbled down the hall, this time to the bathroom. He had me take off my garments so he could see me naked in the mirror.

"Couldn't you see me before?" I asked. "When I was in the shower or something? Spirits aren't blind, are they?"

"It's different now." He took one of my hands and caressed my chest and stomach. He swiped up a tiny drop of cum he'd missed with the towel and put his finger to my lips. "You're really hot," he said, licking my finger.

I took control of my mouth and frowned. "Good grief," I said. "You're not gay, are you?"

Ebenezer laughed. "Most of us down in Outer Darkness are perverts of one kind or another. I've got a couple dozen boyfriends. Though really the designation doesn't mean much when you can't even kiss."

I tried to say "Flip!" but Ebenezer took over my lips and tongue at the last second and made me say "Fuck!" I clapped a hand over my mouth.

What in the world had I gotten myself into?

"I need to get some sleep," I said. It was important to set boundaries. "Church starts at 9:00 in the morning." I expected an argument, but Ebenezer complied easily enough, and we walked back to the bed. We were getting better at walking already.

When the alarm rang at 7:00, I found I couldn't turn it off right away because Ebenezer was using my right hand to beat off again. He really was a pervert. Even at my worst, I never masturbated twice in one day. But perhaps that would calm him down long enough to sit through three hours of church later.

I let Ebenezer learn how to fry an egg, and I let him brush our teeth. I had to take over, though, when we got dressed. He didn't seem able to tie a tie. "And you'd better let me drive," I said as we headed out to the car. "We don't want to end up in jail."

"Ooh," he said, "prison sex."

"Cut it out. We're going to learn more about the gospel today. That's the whole reason you're here."

In the foyer, I saw Gareth and walked over. We clasped our hands together in our usual friendly greeting, but when we did, his smile turned into a frown. He could tell something was wrong. Ebenezer was lousing up the handshake. "You okay, David?"

I shrugged. "Didn't get much sleep."

"Your eyes look different."

"It's the bags under them, I'm sure."

"You don't have any bags."

I sighed. "Look, Gareth, something *is* up. Can you come over to my place after Priesthood meeting?"

Gareth's frown deepened. "Sure, buddy. Sure."

The next three hours were the longest of my life. Ebenezer was getting cocky, trying to answer questions in class. Since he'd never been through the Veil of Forgetfulness, he seemed to know quite a bit, making me look rather arrogant.

He had me roll my eyes twice when the Gospel Doctrine teacher was speaking, and he coughed rudely when the Elders Quorum instructor made a point about the Atonement. I could see Gareth looking at me worriedly. He was going to blow his top when I told him the rest of the story.

Ebenezer took over on the drive home as well, going ten miles over the speed limit. I was going to have to put an end to this sooner rather than later.

"I don't think so," Ebenezer said.

Damn! I forgot he had access to my thoughts now. I wondered why I didn't have access to his until he spoke to me. I felt a shiver. What if he ended up with *more* control over my body than I had? What if I became relegated to the role of spectator, watching Ebenezer's life from the sidelines?

I ran into my apartment and urinated before Gareth arrived. I hadn't dared try using one of the meetinghouse bathrooms.

"You can't realize how good it feels to pee," Ebenezer informed me. "I want to do it outside in the park sometime, too. And maybe take a crap in the Temple Square Visitors' Center."

Oh my God. Oh my God. Oh my God. This was spiraling quickly. What was I going to do?

Gareth knocked on the door a few minutes later, and Ebenezer jumped to let him in. As soon as he was in the door, though, the most horrific, awful, terrifying, abominable thing happened. Ebenezer grabbed Gareth and began kissing him on the mouth.

He started pulling off Gareth's tie while simultaneously trying to pull off ours. He tore Gareth's shirt off. He tore ours off. He yanked Gareth's pants down. He yanked ours down, too.

Ebenezer grabbed Gareth's hand and dragged him to the bedroom where they had sex. It may have been Ebenezer's first time, but he knew enough to dab some hand lotion on Gareth's anus before trying to enter him. I supposed spirits from Outer Darkness hung out in the bedrooms of fornicators sometimes or in theaters where porn movies were shown. I came, and then I flipped my friend over and sucked him off. Then we both lay on our backs, panting.

"I'm sorry," I finally said. "It wasn't my fault. I let a spirit into my body last night after you left, like we talked about. He's the one doing all this."

Gareth didn't say anything.

"I didn't realize he'd be gay. It's not like the guy submitted a resume. But I had to let him have sex, didn't I? Or what was the point of letting him have a body for a few days? Just so he could taste a hot dog and drink a milk shake?"

Gareth still remained silent. I began to wonder if he'd let a spirit in, too, after our discussion last night. Why else would he have allowed Ebenezer to have sex with him so easily?

"Gareth?"

Gareth got up on one elbow and leaned over to kiss me on the mouth. "I hoped you'd come around eventually," he said, "but I never expected you to break from reality to do it."

"Huh?"

"You know perfectly well there's no one else inside you, David."

"But..."

"I love you, you know."

I felt such a sensation of warmth spreading through my body I knew immediately the Holy Ghost was witnessing to me that it was true. A beam of sunlight, I noticed, had come through the window while we were making love and struck the middle of the bed like a spotlight. Now I could hear two birds on a branch outside the window twittering sweetly to each other.

My heart skipped a beat as I realized what Gareth's declaration meant. To my surprise I could tell that Ebenezer had departed the premises at some point. He'd apparently done what he'd come for. But it was also clear Gareth was right about me. Even in his selfishness, Ebenezer had still managed to push me in the right direction.

I felt like I'd saved the life of someone hit by a car and then discovered he was my long-lost brother who could now donate the kidney I needed. Maybe Ebenezer deserved the Atonement now.

Only it looked like Gareth and I would be joining him in Outer Darkness instead.

"I invited someone in last night," I said, "I *wanted* someone in, and I won't feel right until someone else actually *is* inside me." I reached over to caress Gareth's penis. "I want you to go in as deep as possible."

Gareth grabbed the hand lotion and lifted my legs. He kissed me and pushed his way past my sphincter. I understood now why I'd felt so hungry lately to invite another soul into my body. It wasn't good for man to be alone. And with Gareth, there was no awkward learning curve like there'd been with Ebenezer the previous evening.

We moved together as one, as if we'd been doing this all our lives. I lay on my back, calm and happy underneath the heavenly weight of another man. Feeling Gareth thrusting deeper and deeper, I realized one more thing as well. I understood for the first time that Outer Darkness could never be completely dark if the man I loved was there with me.

Fuck the Atonement.

Maybe next week, I could invite Ebenezer back and have him bring one of his boyfriends for Gareth's benefit as well.

The Coroner's Coronary

"Mr. Caulfield," I said, "tell me exactly what happened." I took out my notebook and nodded to my partner, Detective Brody. He nodded in return and pulled the other witness, Mr. Reid, into the kitchen to question him separately. While Mr. Caulfield wiped his forehead with a cloth handkerchief, I quickly surveyed my surroundings.

Everything in the living room seemed to be in place. The furnishings were lush, both the sofa and easy chair covered in suede, a marble pedestal against the wall supporting a figurine of a mother dancing in a circle with her three children. The carpet still bore fresh vacuum tracks. A painting of Jesus standing next to a Mayan temple hung on one wall, while a painting of an old, dying man holding what looked to be gold or brass plates hung on another.

A Bible rested on one of the end tables next to the sofa. Only the wooden inlay coffee table appeared to be slightly displaced, apparently when Mr. Bolton slumped over.

And, of course, there was seventy-five-year-old Mr. Bolton on the floor, the forensics team at work around him. My partner and I wouldn't even be here except that when Mr. Caulfield called 9-1-1, he insisted Mr. Bolton had been poisoned. Otherwise, the first assessment would probably have been that the old man had simply suffered a heart attack.

Though the poison would surely have been found during the autopsy in any event. Mr. Caulfield had merely given us a head start on the investigation. I understood it was even possible that by being the one to alert us to the possibility of murder, he was proactively trying to dissuade us from considering him a suspect.

"Well, Miss Sanford—"

"It's Detective Sanford," I corrected.

"Sure, Detective Sanford, and it's *Bishop* Caulfield." He smiled warmly, but I didn't feel any warmth. "Brother Reid and I came over to Brother Bolton's home tonight to do our Home Teaching."

"Home Teaching?"

"It's a program where someone visits each member of the congregation once a month to make sure everything is okay," Bishop Caulfield explained. "Normally, everyone gets their assignments pretty much at random, but because Brother Bolton and I have been good friends for so many years, I made sure I was assigned to him myself." He smiled that warm smile again. I thought it odd, given that we were here to discuss a probable murder.

I wondered if his handkerchief was even damp.

"Did Mr. Bolton seem agitated or worried about anything?" I asked.

"Brother Bolton was always agitated about his children," Bishop Caulfield answered, a little too quickly. "He may be physically dead now, but his children have all been spiritually dead for years." He shook his head. "That's the real tragedy."

"Oh?"

"Brother Bolton always put the Church first, like I do," Bishop Caulfield continued. "He had his priorities straight. But his kids were a real problem. Morgan is a history professor at the university. Thinks himself a big intellectual. He's always picking at the Church and finding fault. It really broke Brother Bolton's heart."

I wrote it all down.

"Then there's Harper. She's forever going on about women's rights. She attacks the Church all the time, too."

"Attacks?"

"You know, goes to rallies supporting abortion, encourages women to work outside the home, that sort of thing."

"Uh-huh."

"*You* don't support abortion, do you, Detective Sanford?" The bishop's eyes narrowed.

"Please go on, Bishop Caulfield."

"And finally, there's Shaw. He's the youngest, though even he's in his forties now. Anyway, he's the worst of them all. I'd start by questioning him."

"I'm questioning you, Bishop Caulfield," I reminded him. "What's Shaw's problem?"

"He's gay," the bishop replied. "He's caused the most pain to Brother Bolton over these many years, broken his heart again and again. Brother Bolton cut Shaw out of his will first. Then Harper, and then Morgan. They're all cut out of his will now."

"So none of the kids have a financial motive to kill their father," I said.

Bishop Caulfield blinked. "They have the best motive of all," he replied. "They have hate. Hatred and revenge are always a bigger motivator than mere greed."

I wrote Bishop Caulfield's assertions down. "And Mrs. Bolton?"

"Oh, she died years ago." The bishop shook his head. "Died with a broken heart because of her children."

Lots of broken hearts, I noted. Though the bishop seemed surprisingly composed for someone who'd just lost a good friend. But then, in his ecclesiastical position, he probably dealt with grief on a regular basis like I did. I hadn't been devastated when my father died, had I?

"Okay," I said, "so Mr. Bolton didn't get on with his kids. What makes you think one of them killed him?"

The bishop pointed to a small tub of brownies on the coffee table. "Those were on the doorstep when Brother Reid and I arrived tonight. Came with a note that said, 'Just thinking of you.' He thought they were from someone in the Relief Society."

"Relief Society?"

"Our women's organization. There are a couple of widows who've been after him."

"I see." Was a spurned woman behind the murder, I wondered? Or another man who wanted to eliminate the competition? I thought about Riley and who he might be with these days.

"He offered a brownie to each of us, but Brother Reid is a diabetic, and I…" He laughed, patting his stomach. "Well, you can see I don't need any brownies, either. But Brother Bolton ate one, and almost immediately, he grabbed his chest and fell over. He was poisoned, I tell you. One of his kids poisoned him. Shaw is a good cook. He could easily have put something in those brownies."

"Can you give us contact information for Shaw and the other children?" I asked.

"Yes, ma'am. We keep tabs on all our members, even if they're inactive. I can get that for you at the church."

I closed my notebook, and Bishop Caulfield smiled. "Just one more thing," I said.

"Yes?"

"You've told me who *isn't* in the will. Can you tell me who is?"

The bishop shook his head. "He never told me."

"As close as you were?"

He shook his head again.

"Bishop Caulfield, are *you* the beneficiary of Mr. Bolton's will?"

The bishop choked out a laugh. "We were friends, for goodness' sake, not lovers!" He wiped his brow again. "I don't need his money, anyway. I'm a successful businessman. You're welcome to look at my finances. He never told me who he was leaving his money to. I suggested he leave it to the Church or to charity or something useful, but I don't know if that's what he did or not." He held out his hands, palms upward. "There are some things even close friends don't talk about."

"I see."

We wrapped things up, and then Detective Brody and I compared notes in the car while the bishop headed for his office. I summed up what I'd learned, and he reported what Mr. Reid had told him. It seemed that Mr. Bolton had been the county's Medical Examiner for years, having retired a decade ago when his wife died.

I'd only been a detective for eight years, so I didn't remember him. Mr. Reid recalled that the deceased had performed numerous autopsies on murder victims throughout his career—stranglings, shootings, stabbings, staged suicides. Once, about fifteen years ago, one of the murderers physically threatened him after being released from prison.

"We'd better check to see if anyone he helped convict is back on the streets," I said.

"We can always ask if Rebecca's boyfriend heard anything," Det. Brody pointed out.

I scowled in response, not eager to talk about my daughter's living arrangements with an ex-con. "I'm sure he doesn't know every felon in the prison system," I said. "And the guy's been out for a year already."

"It'll give you an excuse to call."

"And you think bringing up her boyfriend's criminal past is the way for us to reconcile?"

"It was just a thought."

It was growing late, but this was a murder investigation, so the victim's children needed to be informed—and questioned—as soon as possible. The bishop called me from the church to give us the addresses for all three suspects, and we stopped to see Shaw Bolton first. His living room was decorated with large, framed photographs of mountains and waterfalls.

The front curtains were a cerulean blue with embroidered cascades coming down. The sound of rushing water played softly in the background. "You don't seem very surprised to hear about your father's death," I noted after we explained what happened.

Shaw gave a wry smile in response. "I haven't seen my father in fifteen years," he said. "I sent him a wedding invitation two years ago, and he didn't even bother to respond. You tell me my dad's dead but that news doesn't change anything in my life. For all I know, he could have died ten years ago along with Mom and my life would still be the same. I don't see any difference hearing the news tonight."

"Uh-huh."

"When the heart stops beating, you die a physical death. But when your heart stops loving…" He closed his eyes and didn't finish the thought.

"Can your partner account for your whereabouts this afternoon and early evening?" I asked.

"He's my husband, not my partner, and no, we don't spend every waking moment together. We were both at work until 5:00—different jobs—and came home after that. I cooked dinner and then we watched TV."

"How long did it take you to get home?"

"Takes me half an hour on most days. Today it took forty minutes."

"I see."

"You think I killed my father?" Shaw asked with a bemused smile.

"This is funny to you?"

"Do you know, when I went to Boys State back in high school, I ran for the office of coroner to please my father. I won, too. And Dad *was* pleased. I was the Golden Boy most of my life. Until I came out. The last thing my father ever said to me was, 'I hope you get AIDS so you can be humbled and repent.'" He chuckled but in a mirthless way. "He didn't say it to be mean, you understand. He was completely sincere. But that only made it hurt more."

"I see."

"So I suppose I had a reason to hate him, but no more reason today than I've had any time over the past fifteen years."

"All right," I said, closing my notebook. "That's all for now, but don't go anywhere for the next several days."

"Ari and I have tickets to fly out to Paris on Wednesday."

Det. Brody and I exchanged glances. "Plan on canceling the trip," I said.

He frowned. "If you insist."

On our way to see Mr. Bolton's daughter, Det. Brody and I reflected on what we'd just learned. "He didn't seem very broken up about the murder, did he?" asked Det. Brody.

"Can you blame him?"

"Do you think he planned the trip to France as a way to escape?" he persisted.

"If he'd wanted to do that, wouldn't the tickets have been purchased for tonight?"

Det. Brody scratched his chin. "Didn't you notice the lingering smell of baked goods in the house?"

"He's a cook," I said. "He bakes."

I tried to come up with a rough theory during the remainder of the drive, but I didn't have enough information yet.

Harper Bolton had apparently already heard about her father's murder by the time we arrived. She opened the door two seconds after we knocked. "Let's get this over with," she said, ushering us in. I noticed her living room was filled with abstract and modern art. One sculpture on the top shelf of a waist high bookcase was a simple black cube. A thick, rectangular sheet of silver metal, perhaps nickel or steel, was bolted to one wall at a slight angle.

"Do you know anyone who might have wanted to harm your father?" I asked once we were seated.

"Not really," she replied. "My father and I didn't get along that well, but most people loved him. Sister Phillips from the Relief Society called to let me know what happened. I don't go to church anymore, but I let the Visiting Teachers keep in touch with me."

"When was the last time you talked with your father?"

"Last weekend. We usually get together every Saturday just to chat over a doughnut." She patted her belly. "I got my mother's genes. My father is still as fit as he was at twenty."

"Was as fit."

Harper nodded. "Dad and I had a strained relationship, as I'm sure the bishop was happy to tell you. My father wouldn't let me talk about my work at Planned Parenthood or any protests I took part in. I wouldn't permit him to talk about church. He didn't like the 'decadent' movies I saw. I didn't like the pablum he watched on television. Basically, our conversation was relegated to discussing which commercials we liked or disliked."

"I see."

"He hated the ads for erectile dysfunction. Or constipation. Or those about catheters."

"Someone with his medical background?"

"It was all about propriety," Harper said. "He liked commercials about fabric whiteners." She rolled her eyes. "I'm not kidding."

"Did seeing your father every week make you angry?" I asked. "Being constantly reminded of the differences between you two?"

Harper laughed. "I was cut out of the will ages ago. We all were. Your best bet is to follow the money. Who *does* benefit from his death?"

"He never told you who he left his money and assets to?"

"Nope. And I didn't ask. It was his money to do with as he pleased."

"Uh-huh."

Det. Brody and I wrapped up the meeting and headed over to see the remaining son. It was really getting late now, almost 10:45, but I wanted to talk to Morgan before he had any more time to cover his tracks. If he had any tracks, that is. Morgan lived in a smallish house in a working-class neighborhood with grass a little too tall in front. Once inside, all I could see were bookcases crammed with books.

I quickly perused the shelves while Morgan made us some coffee. A good many of the books were mystery novels, I noted. The kind of books which often explained in detail how to commit murder. Most of the other volumes were history books and various academic tomes, some of them analyzing the mystery genre.

"I was home alone since I finished my office hours around 3:00," Morgan volunteered, handing me a steaming cup of black coffee.

"So your whereabouts are unaccounted for this afternoon and evening?" I asked.

"You got it."

"Did you kill your father?"

Morgan laughed. "Why would I kill him? I'm not in the will. Dad made that clear almost every time we talked. He was always offering to change it, of course, if I would just repent."

"Repent of what?"

"Of basing my life on facts instead of feelings." He chuckled, though the sound he made wasn't light. "He couldn't forgive us, and we couldn't forgive him. I think that's made all of us a little dead inside for a long time." He sighed. "But I didn't finish him off."

The children were making good points, I conceded. While they all spoke of the will with a tinge of bitterness, it seemed unlikely that any of them was the killer. This despite the fact that most murders were committed by family members. Unless there'd been some development with their father that no one was mentioning, I couldn't find a precipitating event. "Do you know anyone who might have a motive?" I asked.

Morgan shrugged. "He was well-liked at church, from what I can tell. But my father and I didn't talk all that often. He seemed to be softening a bit toward us lately, but if he was, it was at such a slow pace I didn't have the patience to wait around for it. I haven't spoken to him in a couple of months."

After we left the last child's home, Det. Brody and I called it quits for the day. I went back to my place, undressed, and looked at my cell phone for a long while, my finger poised over the numbers. Why was Rebecca foolishly ruining her life, I wondered, deliberately tying herself to a convicted criminal? Was it just to spite me?

I brushed my teeth, washed my face, and then fell into bed, still feeling dirty. I dreamed about my own father, to whom I'd never been close. We'd become even more distant as he grew older and developed dementia, accusing me of stealing from him. We hadn't spoken in over a year when I learned two months ago he had died.

I wished Riley hadn't left me—what was it, nine years ago now? Rebecca needed more than just me, but Riley had abandoned her, too.

Three cups of strong coffee and a hot shower Saturday morning had me ready to resume the case. I called Bishop Caulfield and asked if there were any members of his congregation I could talk to. He gave me several names, and Det. Brody and I started on our second day of questioning.

"Mr. Thompson," I said when a middle-aged gentleman opened the door, "I'm Det. Sanford and this is my partner, Det. Brody."

"Bishop Caulfield told me what happened."

"Can we come in?"

He ushered us into his living room. The décor reminded me of the murder victim's home, a painting of Jesus surrounded by children on the wall behind the sofa, and a photo of the Salt Lake temple on another wall. Even as a disinterested agnostic, I knew enough about Mormons to recognize that edifice. "I suppose the bishop told you I wasn't the biggest fan of Brother Bolton."

Det. Brody and I exchanged glances. "Tell us about it."

"Well, I teach Gospel Doctrine every Sunday," Mr. Thompson continued. "Brother Bolton had become an increasing distraction in class, asking difficult questions all the time."

"A troublemaker?" asked Det. Brody.

Mr. Thompson shrugged. "Not really," he said. "He wasn't *trying* to be a pain in the butt." He paused. "Excuse the language. But he made the other members very uncomfortable. A couple of them even stopped coming to church altogether. He was becoming a big problem."

"Sounds like a motive to me," I said. Albeit a minor one.

Mr. Thompson held up his hand. "I was doing research to help him," he protested. "I know some people feel that once you start to doubt, you're already too far gone to repent, but Brother Bolton was salvageable. If you want to know who had a grudge against him, talk to Brother Tedesco."

That was one of the other names Bishop Caulfield had provided. "And what is his relationship with the victim?"

"Brother Tedesco is the High Priests Group Leader. Brother Bolton was a high priest."

I felt the hairs on the back of my neck prick up. The title sounded creepy rather than impressive, making me think of rituals and robes and long, thin knives. But I wasn't here to investigate the religion.

Det. Brody and I drove over to meet with the High Priests Group Leader next and got right to the point. "I hear you didn't like Mr. Bolton," I began.

Mr. Tedesco's jaw tightened. "I didn't kill him," he said stiffly, "although I had every right to."

"And why is that?"

"He was after my wife."

Det. Brody and I exchanged glances. "Can you account for your whereabouts yesterday afternoon and evening?" I asked.

"I was at work until 5:30. I came home for a quick dinner, and then I went out to do my Home Teaching."

"You guys do a lot of Home Teaching," I observed.

"It's the end of the month."

I wasn't quite sure how that point was relevant, but I let it pass. "Can anyone confirm this?" I asked.

"My Home Teaching companion, of course." He provided the name.

"Can we speak to your wife privately?"

Mr. Tedesco scowled but called in his wife and then left the room. Mrs. Tedesco was short and rather heavy, not the normal object of an illicit affair, but I'd seen it happen before. She was a good two decades younger than Mr. Bolton. For some men, that would be enough.

"What was your relationship with the deceased?" I asked.

"Just friends," she replied, clasping her hands together tightly, her fingernails digging into her skin. She turned to look down the hall, presumably to make sure her husband wasn't eavesdropping.

"Why does your husband think Mr. Bolton was interested in you?"

"Oh, dear, must we talk about this? It's all so… so…unpalatable."

I smiled. "Murder often is."

Mrs. Tedesco looked down the hall again. "*Please* don't say anything to my husband, but…"

"Yes?"

"I saw Brother Bolton privately several times in the past few months."

"Were you having an affair?"

"Goodness no! He was asking about my sister."

"He wanted to date your sister?" Why in the world couldn't she relate that information to her husband? Something wasn't adding up.

"My sister is a lesbian."

Now I was really confused.

"Brother Bolton was trying to understand homosexuality. One of his sons is gay, you know."

I nodded.

"Brother Bolton seemed to have a lot of difficulty with Shaw, but he truly loved that boy." She sighed. "I wish Brother Bolton had just talked to the bishop about it. They were always so close. But he wanted to talk to me." She paused. "I think Brother Bolton was almost ready to make up with his son."

Just Shaw, I wondered? This was news. I frowned, wondering if the other two kids were aware of this. "So why don't you want your husband to know?"

"He hates my sister. She was excommunicated, you see."

I made a mental note that Mrs. Tedesco's explanation still didn't clear her husband of the murder, since he wasn't fully aware of the actual circumstances. Det. Brody nudged me and pointed to his cell. There was a text from the lab confirming that the brownies had indeed been laced with poison. Digoxin, to be specific, a form of digitalis found in foxglove. "May we take a look around your yard, Mrs. Tedesco?"

"My yard?" Her eyebrows furrowed. "Certainly."

As I suspected, there were pink, yellow, and purple foxglove about the property.

"Why are you looking at my flowers?"

I put my notebook away. "We may be back later for more questioning. You and Mr. Tedesco should stay home today."

"All right, Officer."

"Detective."

In the car, Det. Brody summarized. "Motive and weapon but also an alibi." He wrinkled his nose and opened his notebook to the next address on the list while I tried to make sense of everything we'd heard so far. We talked to a couple of Mr. Bolton's neighbors and a few more members from his congregation, two of them widows.

All anyone could tell us was that he was a "very nice man," "very devout," and "very neighborly." Apparently, he was "very" everything. Records at the precinct showed that no one convicted as a result of the coroner's findings had been released within the last year.

Det. Brody and I made the rounds of the three children once again. Both Shaw and Morgan also had foxglove growing in their gardens. Of course, it was a common flower in this region. A thousand people across the city probably grew them. I remembered a case a couple of years ago where a victim had been murdered gruesomely with a butter knife, and how maddening it had been to realize that every household in the city potentially housed the murder weapon.

During our second round of interviews, Shaw asked if he could see his father. Harper had no interest in doing so, and Morgan wanted to wait a little longer.

"Feeling guilty?" I asked.

"Yes," he admitted.

"Do tell."

"If only I could have gotten through to him, but I just kept losing my patience. Shaw won't admit it, but he still loved our father. Harper and I were never as close to Dad as he was."

"Did you feel distant enough to be able to kill him?"

He shrugged. "Probably. I've always been more analytical than emotional."

"I'll repeat my question from last night," I said. "Did you kill your father?"

"He was going to change his will," Morgan replied. "I don't have any proof of that, but I'm almost sure of it. It might have been six months or a year away, but he was coming around. Not that that would have helped us get along any better. But if I was going to kill him, I'd have waited a little longer."

"Or maybe you just learned that he refused to *ever* change his will," I suggested, "and it made you angry because you'd been hoping he would finally give you some money." I noticed the fabric on the arm of the sofa was fraying.

"Have you found out who *is* the beneficiary?" he asked. "I sure don't know. Harper said she asked you to look into it."

"We called your father's attorney this morning," Det. Brody said. "She was in the country for the weekend but agreed to come back and get us a copy of the will today. We're going to her office right now."

"Logic says whoever is about to be cut out of the inheritance is the person who killed my father."

I kept my face impassive as we said our goodbyes. Det. Brody and I did go next to the attorney's office. She looked none too pleased to be there. She quickly handed us a copy of the will and then ushered us out of the office, locking it behind her. Det. Brody and I sat in the car and read.

"He's left everything to the Mormon Church," I said. "It's not going to another person at all." This didn't clear up anything.

"Well, the Mormon Church certainly didn't kill him," Det. Brody replied with a laugh.

I thought for a moment. "Let's talk to the bishop one more time," I suggested. "Maybe he can shed some light on the situation." My mind raced almost as much as my heart on the drive over as I kept trying to piece everything together.

"Mr. Caulfield," I said as we sat down in the bishop's living room, "thanks for seeing us again." There was a painting of wagons crossing the plains on one wall. On another wall hung a painting showing a beam of light descending through some trees and striking a kneeling teenager, who had his arm raised to shield himself from the glare. The living room itself was probably 700 square feet. He hadn't been lying about having money.

"It's Bishop," he replied.

"Yes, Mr. Caulfield, I understand." I looked at Det. Brody, who frowned in response.

"My wife's out doing her Visiting Teaching," the bishop offered.

"She was gone yesterday afternoon as well?" I ventured.

The bishop didn't respond.

"You've told us you were very close to Mr. Bolton. One of your congregants confirmed that assessment. I expect you talked about almost everything together. Including that will."

The bishop was frowning now, too.

"May we see your back yard?"

"Huh?"

I repeated the question, and Mr. Caulfield led us out back. "I see you've cut one of your foxglove," I said.

"I—I gave it to a neighbor," he stammered. "She liked the color."

"Do you often give flowers to women other than your wife?"

Mr. Caulfield's lips tightened.

"I'm sure DNA analysis will show that *your* foxglove is the source of the poison that killed your good friend." The least he could have done, I thought, was take it from someone else's yard. Or did he simply think God would feel obligated to protect him? "Would you care to explain?"

"I want to speak to my lawyer."

"Mr. Caulfield, I'm going to call the precinct while you call your attorney. When everyone gets here, we'll have a nice, long chat about Mr. Bolton's inheritance, and how you always put the Church first." The bishop looked as if he was about to protest. "We can either talk here or at the station." I smiled, but I expected Mr. Caulfield didn't feel any warmth.

All this misery, I thought, because a father was too proud to accept his children for who they were. Such a senseless tragedy, even without the murder.

After he made his call, Mr. Caulfield sat on the sofa, staring mutely at the painting of the beam of light. Det. Brody spent his time sending texts. But I could only think about one thing, the only truly important concern in this whole experience.

While we waited, I walked to the kitchen and pulled out my cell phone, my heart pounding. I took a deep breath and gave Rebecca a call.

Twenty-Six Years

Susan wanted to see it. She couldn't believe it was even here in a video store in Hattiesburg. Small towns in Mississippi weren't known for progressive thinking, even if they were university towns like hers. Susan glanced down again and, looking around to see that no one was watching, she picked up the DVD. *Latter Days*.

Alan would be upset if he saw she'd rented it. He was more homophobic than she was. She'd been shocked ten years ago when her nephew, Jeff, had told her he was gay and had been excommunicated, but she still loved him. Alan always told her in private he knew Jeff was going to hell, though he tried to be nice to Jeff in person.

Susan didn't know if her nephew was going to hell or not. Probably he was, but she didn't treat him any differently now that she knew. She could be open-minded.

Susan decided she'd have to watch *Latter Days* sometime before Alan came home from work. Maybe tomorrow she'd teach half a day and then go home sick. She could watch the movie alone before Laura, her youngest, got home from high school. Anna was in college now and rarely around the house, and the two oldest children had married in the temple and lived away from home. She'd be safe.

When Susan reached the head of the line, she put the two DVDs she was renting on the counter. The other movie was

Kate and Leopold. The clerk, a bored-looking girl about eighteen, scanned the DVDs. "It's for a project," Susan explained, meaning the gay movie. Then she felt like an idiot. The girl didn't say anything but put the two movies in a bag.

Out in the parking lot, Susan slipped the DVD of *Latter Days* into her purse and left the other in the bag. She hoped the second movie would be okay. Laura and Anna were too big for things like *Stuart Little* and *Shrek*, so it was hard to find movies they could watch as a family. *Kate and Leopold* was fairly innocuous. It was a love story, and Susan had seen it at the theater by herself a few years ago, unable to resist Hugh Jackman.

She didn't remember there being a sex scene. One hardly paid attention anymore, but she wanted her girls to wait until marriage as she had, so the less temptation the better. Movies too often made sex seem like fun, and that wasn't good for married people, much less kids. That was why the Church forbid R-rated movies even for adults.

Back home, Susan quickly cut up some fresh broccoli and lightly cooked that in the microwave while she boiled some spaghetti and heated some Ragu. Alan had served a mission in Milan twenty-eight years ago and wanted pasta at least twice a week, and the kids never seemed to mind.

Her oldest, Steven, had gone to Peru on a mission. He was now second counselor in the ward bishopric, not bad for a twenty-five-year-old, but Susan still thought him just as immature as before his mission, even with a baby daughter now. He'd just graduated from college and gotten his first real job as an accountant. He seemed like he'd have a good life, though, and that was a relief.

The oldest girl, Becky, had said all through her teens she would also serve a mission, but Susan had known it would never happen. She liked boys too much. Susan's biggest disappointment was the year Becky went to New Orleans for Mardi Gras and came back drunk.

As far as Susan knew, though, it was the only time her daughter ever drank. Becky soon married in the Baton Rouge temple like her brother, and she'd just finished nursing school and moved to St. Louis to work in a critical care unit there. Susan wished Becky could have stayed closer to home, but St. Louis was where her husband got a job, so that's where they went. No kids yet. Susan hoped they wouldn't wait too long. After all, having children was more important than being a nurse.

Susan set the table and called the others in for dinner. Even though Anna was in college now, she still ate dinner with the family, which was nice. She had friends from a sorority, and Susan suspected that Anna had gone drinking with them a few times, but she'd never come home drunk, so that was something.

She'd dated a nonmember for several months and gotten him to join the Church, but then a few months later she'd dumped him. Yet Susan still had hope she'd marry in the Church. An eternal marriage was the single most important thing you could do in this life.

"Spaghetti!" Alan said happily, sitting down a moment later. "Looks good."

"And broccoli!" said Laura. It was one of the few vegetables she liked.

"I always aim to please."

"Your turn to say the prayer, Anna," said Alan. They all bowed their heads while Anna offered a blessing on the food.

"Anything interesting happen today?" Alan asked. The question was directed to no one in particular.

Susan wasn't about to mention she'd rented what was probably an anti-Mormon film, but that fact so overwhelmed her she could hardly think of anything else to say. She forced herself to think of the fourth grade class she taught. "One of my students misspelled his name again."

"What's new?" said Anna. She swallowed a piece of broccoli and then added, "I gave another speech in speech class. The other students get so scared, but I've been giving talks in church all my life, so it's no big deal."

"Well, we don't learn chemistry at church," Laura said, "and I'm studying my brains out just to make a B. I hate it."

Laura was in eleventh grade and wanted to graduate in the top 3% of her class next year like her siblings had all done. She generally made A's and was never happy with a B, and that made Susan proud. The public schools here were not all that demanding, she knew, but an A was an A.

"Science is good," Alan said. "You can always get a job in the sciences." He himself worked with computers at the university. He didn't really like it, but their kids all received free tuition, so Susan knew he planned to stay until Laura graduated college.

"Who wants a job in chemistry?" asked Laura.

"You could do drug research," said Alan. "You know Grandma is always in pain because of her arthritis. You could develop better pain medicine. Or you could develop treatments for cancer. Or find a cure for AIDS."

"Who wants to find a cure for AIDS? 99% of the people who have it get it from sinning."

"So you'll let the other 1% die for spite?" Alan asked. Susan knew he didn't really care about people with AIDS, either. When Jeff told them a few years ago he'd contracted HIV just before he met Devon, Alan had been sympathetic in person but had afterward told Susan, "The wages of sin is death." He was challenging Laura now simply because he liked to play Devil's advocate to keep the girls sharp. She liked that about him.

"I just think there are more important diseases to cure first."

"So you're saying drug research *is* a possibility?"

"Oh, good grief."

They went on to discuss other things. Anna talked of a boy in one of her classes who kept asking for help with the coursework. She couldn't decide if he was interested in her or just really stupid. Alan talked of having to instruct a professor yet again on how to use Blackboard to post assignments for his students.

Susan had nothing to offer. After three years as Relief Society president, she now had no callings at church, for the first time in as long as she could remember. So that took away lots of topics for conversation. And teaching was always just the same old thing. They'd found a knife in one of her students' backpacks last week, but that was old news.

One of her fellow teachers was discovered to be having an extramarital affair with the school nurse, but Susan didn't want to say anything that might make the girls think about sex. She wanted to talk about the movie in her purse, which would be even worse, so she didn't dare.

As the girls were clearing the table, the phone rang, and Susan answered it. "Hi, Sharon," she said, recognizing her friend's voice. Sharon taught in the room next to Susan's.

"I don't know what I'm going to do!" Sharon moaned into the phone.

"What's wrong?"

"Someone shot at our house. I'm sure it was because of Kenny." Kenny was Sharon's teenage son who was into drugs. Thank God Susan had the Church and didn't have to worry about things like that.

"Was anyone hurt?"

"No. Just a hole in the front door. Susan, I can't take this much longer. What am I going to do?"

Kick him out, Susan wanted to say. That's what she'd do if someone in her family was breaking the law. It would be a sign of love. Tough love, maybe, a little cold, perhaps, but still love. "Can you get him into rehab?" Susan asked.

"He won't go. I'm afraid he's going to get Pete into drugs." Pete was Sharon's twelve-year-old.

"Sharon, you have to do something. You could get killed. Pete could get killed." Susan felt a little flushed to be saying this, watching the reaction of her girls as they overheard her end of the conversation. It was terrible the way lives could fall apart so easily without the Church. But it gave her a kind of thrill to be so near it.

Near but far. Maybe she was getting too close by renting that movie. But she'd worry about that later.

"Oh, you're right," Sharon said. "What in the world am I going to do?"

"Did you call the police?"

"Oh, I can't! They'd want to know why someone was shooting at us. They might search the house. God only knows what they'd find in Kenny's room."

"Can't he go live with his father?"

"His father doesn't want him. That's why he's into drugs in the first place."

They talked a few more minutes, but there was really nothing useful Susan could suggest. "Tell him to repent!" she wanted to say. Kenny wasn't even nice. You could put up with a lot of sin if the person was at least nice. It made her want to be doubly sure her girls were safe, so after she hung up, Susan talked about how bad drugs were, without actually coming out and asking if Anna and Laura had ever tried them.

You couldn't act suspicious, or that might drive kids away. But both girls made appropriately disapproving comments about drugs, so Susan felt okay.

After everyone had moved to the living room, Susan showed them the movie she'd rented for tonight, and they all settled down to watch *Kate and Leopold*. It was pure romantic fluff but sweet. Hugh Jackman stood up every time Meg Ryan left the table. Susan remembered that at the beginning of their marriage twenty-six years ago, Alan had opened the car door for her every day. That had lasted about three years before he gave it up.

"I wish I could go back in time like Meg Ryan," said Anna. "Men are such dogs these days."

"Men were—" Susan stopped herself. She'd almost said that men were always dogs, but that wouldn't sound right. So she said, "There are some good men today. You only need one."

"Is Hugh Jackman married?" Laura asked, laughing.

"Afraid so." Susan had learned that when she looked up his name on the web. It wasn't that she lusted after other men. She really wasn't interested in sex at all. She and Alan hadn't had sex in seven years now.

But every once in a while a good-looking man did catch her eye. She didn't think of sex when she saw one, though. It was more like simply appreciating a nice work of art.

"Mom, you got a minute?" Laura asked later as Susan was brushing her teeth.

Susan spit into the sink and turned to Laura. "What's up?"

Laura looked at her feet and kicked at the floor. Susan's stomach knotted. It wasn't about sex, was it?

"You know you can tell me anything." Susan could feel her pulse beating faster, but she kept a blank face.

"Well…"

"What is it? Something at school?" Maybe someone had offered her a cigarette.

"No," said Laura. "Well, kind of."

"It has to do with a teacher?" Had someone made a pass at her? She'd kill him.

"No."

"With a friend at school?" Did some boy grope her in the hall? She'd kill him, too.

Laura didn't say anything, so it must have something to do with a friend. But what had happened? Susan liked that her kids had always been able to come to her, but sometimes it was like pulling teeth to find out things.

"What'd your friend say?" Better to start with "say" and then move on to "do."

"Well, she was looking for something in her brother's room. And she found some magazines."

Oh, Lord.

"It was these women doing all sorts of terrible things. It really upset Jennifer. She wants to know if she should tell her parents. What do you think?"

"She should tell them right away. Pornography is addictive. That boy will only get worse. No telling what will happen if he keeps looking at that stuff."

"But her brother'll get mad if she tells."

"He'll never be a good husband if he looks at that crap. Jennifer won't only be helping her brother. She'll be helping her brother's wife when he gets married."

Laura was quiet a minute. Susan didn't know if she'd been too harsh. That sometimes turned kids off.

No, kids liked to have limits. And you definitely had to limit sex.

But why was Laura so quiet?

"Mom?"

"Yes?"

"Why are guys so…so sick?"

"I think it's genetic," Susan said slowly. Then she frowned. "Or maybe their spirits are different to begin with, right from the Pre-Existence. I don't know. That's probably why men need the priesthood to begin with. They're weaker. Just be glad you're a girl. We get cramps, but at least we aren't…"

"Perverts," said Laura.

"Right."

"Mom?"

"Yes?"

"Dad's not like that, is he? And Steven?"

"No, they're not like that."

"What about cousin Jeff?"

Susan shrugged. Jeff and Devon seemed pretty clean cut except for the gay thing. Neither of them smoked or drank. She hoped Jeff wasn't depraved in addition to being gay. Somehow, he seemed okay. If it was anyone else, she'd be more judgmental. But she liked Jeff. They connected.

"I don't think so."

"I hope not, or I'll never speak to him again. Dad doesn't like him anyway."

"You better get to bed."

"Good night, Mom."

Back in her room, Susan put on her nightgown and watched Alan strip to his garments. She'd never approved of sleeping in just her Mormon underwear, but Alan always did it, even though he knew she disapproved. It irritated her. Tonight, she wasn't going to worry about it, though. In fact, once she was in bed, all she could think about was the DVD in her purse.

She felt guilty for sinning, but there was something exciting about it, too. She'd never smoked and never drank, but she had once gone alone to a coffeehouse and ordered a latte. It hadn't been all that good, but to taste it was still thrilling. She'd never told the bishop about it, but she'd skipped taking the sacrament the following Sunday.

Lying in bed, Susan thought back to the time she was Laura's age. She'd been a good student, too. And she'd always enjoyed church. She'd read the Book of Mormon cover to cover when she was fifteen, and she'd had a testimony ever since. She'd never really considered going on a mission, but she knew she'd only marry a returned missionary.

She'd met Alan at Institute on the University of Southern Mississippi campus in Hattiesburg. He always participated in class and always knew the right answers. He had a good sense of humor and seemed overall like a decent guy. They'd become friends first and only later did Alan ask to date her. He was always a perfect gentleman, and when he proposed, Susan knew she'd never find anyone better.

They'd gone to Washington, DC to get married, that being the closest temple to Mississippi back then. That was twenty-six years ago.

Susan still remembered their wedding night, surely one of the most awful moments of her life. Alan had climbed on top of her and started pumping away. It seemed to take forever and was getting more boring by the minute. Susan had been thoroughly confused. Wasn't this supposed to be exciting? Wasn't this supposed to be fun? Why all the warnings against premarital sex if it was so unpleasant?

When Alan finally finished and plopped down beside her, he'd asked, "Did you come?" Susan didn't even know what that meant. But when she finally figured it out, she felt cheated.

Not once in all their years of lovemaking had she ever experienced an orgasm. Susan wasn't sure if Alan just wasn't doing it right or if something was wrong with her. She thought of trying to masturbate to see if she could stimulate herself, to see if she was physically capable of a climax, but that would be sinning.

So she became less and less interested in sex as the years went by. Once, about nine or ten years into their marriage, she and Alan were in the drugstore and Alan jokingly pointed to a 36-count box of condoms. "We should get it for our year's supply."

"That's a three-year supply," she had responded immediately, not wanting him to get any ideas.

In the beginning, Alan had pestered her for more sex, but thankfully he'd gradually gotten used to the fact that there wasn't going to be much. Susan had wanted to cuddle at first, but it seemed cuddling was always followed by an attempt at sex, and when she had pointed this out to Alan, he'd looked hurt and started staying on his side of the bed.

But after a while, Susan no longer missed the cuddling. Then had come the day seven years ago when Alan had come to her with the big announcement. He was gay. Just like Jeff. He hadn't ever had sex with a man and he wasn't going to, but it was a secret he didn't feel he could keep any longer. He simply wanted her to know.

Strangely, Susan didn't feel either shock or revulsion at the news. What she felt was relief. "Thank god," she told him. "Now we don't have to have sex anymore."

She never thought of divorcing him. Why should she? He was a good man. He was Seminary instructor at church, paid his tithing, and was basically good to her. He'd been a stake missionary for years and Gospel Doctrine teacher for a while, too. He'd never been ordained a high priest, which was disappointing, but he didn't like leadership roles, anyway. He still wrote regularly to the five people he baptized in Italy.

But she had to see that movie about the gay Mormon missionary. What if? What if Alan had "come out," as they called it, instead of marrying her? What if she'd married someone else? She had good kids. She couldn't complain there. And that was saying something in this day and age. But she might have had good kids with someone else, too.

And really, she wondered sometimes if that was enough. Once, she'd learned about a woman in the ward who was raped years ago and became pregnant. The woman kept the baby and loved her, because the baby was innocent and deserved to be loved, and she always seemed happy with the girl, who was so sweet even as a teenager.

But could having a child you truly loved ever possibly mean the rape was a good thing? Susan was glad to have helped save Alan's soul, but she still wondered if that meant it was *right* for him to have married her. Fair.

Kind.

Yet maybe if he wasn't going to be satisfied with a woman anyway, it was good she wasn't interested in sex with him, either.

Maybe they *were* right for each other. And she had to admit, knowing he was gay somehow made her life a little more daring, more dangerous. She wasn't like all the other, average women at church.

But Susan had often felt a little distant from Alan, good as he was. If she could feel close to Jeff, why not to Alan as well? She always smiled at church, and people thought she was happy. But what would it have been like to be with a man who fully loved her? Not for the sex. She didn't care about the sex. But just to feel truly and completely loved.

And maybe—what the heck—maybe the sex would in fact have been good. She couldn't help but feel she'd missed out on a basic part of her earthly existence. Sex was all anyone ever talked about. It *must* be good.

What would it have been like to enjoy it even once?

She sighed and turned over, still thinking, but eventually fell asleep.

Around 5:00, Susan woke up thirsty. She thought about waiting till the alarm went off at 6:00 to get something to drink but then decided she couldn't wait. She was going to try to get out of bed without waking Alan but then saw that he wasn't in bed. He must have gone to the bathroom. Susan got up and walked toward the kitchen, but as she passed the den, she saw a light flickering.

She peeked in and saw Alan watching TV, the volume low. That was odd. He hardly ever had insomnia. Then she saw what was on the screen. Two young men were in a restaurant kissing. What the—?

Susan stood behind Alan and watched as the last few minutes of the movie unfolded. When the credits started rolling, Alan removed the disk and put it back in the case. Only then did he see Susan.

"How long have you been there?"

"A few minutes."

"I had an upset stomach. I couldn't find any Tums and so I looked in your purse."

"I was going to watch it this afternoon before you came home from work."

"No, I think we should all watch it tonight after dinner."

"You mean you want the kids to see it?"

"I think they should."

"Was there any sex in the movie?"

"Yes. There was sex."

Susan was silent a moment. "Okay."

"Someday, they'll have to know, one way or another."

"You think that's wise?"

Alan laughed. "Wise? Who knows? You've been very good to me for a very long time, but it's hard to live without love. I know it's wrong, but I just get so lonely. I'll try to wait at least until Laura is in college. Maybe no one will even want me. But I think at some point I'll have to try."

Susan nodded but didn't say anything. So this was it, she realized dully. She'd be getting a temple divorce. She wouldn't be going to the Celestial Kingdom. You could get there by yourself, she supposed, but she knew she wouldn't. Somehow, even with all those years of work, she'd lost. She thought she'd feel a little thrill if this day ever came, but there was nothing.

Then she wondered briefly that if she started dating in the future sometime, she might need to have sex with someone else.

"You okay?"

She nodded again, the corners of her mouth turning upward just slightly. "I'm thirsty," she said. "I'm going to get something to drink."

Counting Nozzles

"Oh, shoot! I forgot the nozzles!" I said, reaching for the door handle.

I quickly walked past the two pump islands in front of the Gulf station and counted. Four pumps and six nozzles. They'd get a three rating. Not bad, since the highest was five.

"Come on, Gray," Wanda said almost in a whine as I sat back down in the car. "You're getting slower on each one. I want to finish and get home."

I didn't tell her that if she'd parked in a better position I wouldn't have had to get out of the car again. But she did have a point. After a week and a half of surveying gas stations, I shouldn't be forgetting such obvious points. It had been a long day, though. We'd finished fourteen outlets before lunch and five since then.

We were ahead of schedule and I didn't feel like killing myself just because Wanda needed to get home early to buy some fabric she'd forgotten to get the day before.

I picked up the portable computer and put it on my lap. Snapping open the cover, I called up the first panel and began entering in the information I'd gathered. Fortunately, Wanda didn't talk when I was on the machine. She'd sing along with the radio or read the scriptures, but at least she didn't talk.

Wanda was a nice enough woman, but she'd been griping all day. I had half the money for my ticket to Austria, though, so putting up with her was at least profitable.

The first three panels in the computer needed little correction, but I had to add in the new fuel prices and new hours that had changed since the survey done two years before. I also had to guess on the volume of gasoline pumped each month because the manager hadn't wanted to tell me for fear that we'd use the information against him.

I hoped my work wasn't being used to hurt people. I did get the job, after all, through the Church.

"One more thing," I said, hopping out of the car again. What was the matter with me today? I was forgetting everything. I checked the price for the car wash and then headed back.

"I thought you were through," said the attendant I'd talked with earlier.

"Almost." I smiled.

"Is that your wife in the car?" he asked. "I'd like to work with mine, too."

"Oh, no," I said, laughing. "Just friends." I shuddered as I walked back to the car. Wanda was just another member of my congregation, and much older than I was as well.

"All finished?" Wanda asked as I closed the computer a minute later. She put the car in reverse and began backing out.

"Yes." I was a little irritated that she always left before I could look up the next address.

"I need to get that fabric today if I'm going to finish Sister Martin's wedding dress by Saturday, so we need to hurry."

I opened the plot map given me by the company and then compared it with a map of the Westbank. They'd sent me to the one part of New Orleans I knew nothing about, but I was learning fast, having to visit all 179 gas outlets on this side of the river.

"The next one is on the corner of Lapalco and Belle Chasse." I folded the maps in half and put them back above the dashboard.

"I have to get a picture of this one first," Wanda said. She pulled out of the station and crossed Lapalco. Then she turned around, and as she approached the station again, she got out her Polaroid camera, stopped the car in the middle of the street, and took a picture. Then Wanda put the car in drive and we headed for the next station. "I hope this one has a bathroom," she said. "I'll be floating soon."

"Yeah."

"And I hope it's got toilet paper."

"You should have picked some up at my house this morning."

"I'm telling ya!" She laughed. "Who did that to your place?"

"I don't know yet."

I did, though. It was my fifteen-year-old stepbrother, Dean. Up until now, we'd gotten along well in the nine months my dad and his mom had been married. We'd played basketball in the afternoon, not because I particularly liked the game but because I wanted to spend time with him. We also discussed the Middle East, homelessness, AIDS, gay rights, and anything else in the news.

I remembered that when I was his age, no one felt I was grown enough to talk about the news. But how old did you have to be to deserve being able to talk about life? Besides, I suspected Dean might be gay and need someone to talk to. I was gay myself though I certainly hadn't told him or anyone else about it.

But I knew how to be supportive if Dean dropped any hints. I could encourage him to abstain and go on a mission as I had. Then he'd be strong enough to stay in the Church and get married. I'd feel I'd accomplished something good in my life that might make up for my own gayness.

I certainly hadn't baptized many people in Austria. So whether or not we were friends because we could both sense the same thing in each other, or for whatever other reason, we did seem to get along better than most step-siblings.

At church, though, Dean and I never let on that we got along because I was his Sunday School teacher, and it wouldn't have been cool for his friends to know he liked the teacher. But at home, we even planned a six-month anniversary party for our parents together.

Then last week my dad finally insisted on a separation after having considered it for three months. Louise started looking for an apartment right away, and Dean left immediately to stay with friends. He hadn't spoken to me since, as if the break up were somehow my fault.

I worried that the separation would drive him away from the Church, that he'd hate the Church as well as us. I knew Dean was sometimes spiteful, having TP'ed the homes of some classmates at school he didn't like, but I'd still been surprised to see the rolls of white toilet paper all over our yard this morning. I was sure he'd done it.

"How did your kids react to your divorce, Wanda?" I asked suddenly. No one knew of the separation yet, so I hoped she wouldn't grow suspicious. My dad didn't want to broadcast his private life, but I suspected Louise was already beginning to spread the news of how she'd been "kicked out of the house."

"Oh, pretty well," she replied. "Rob was such a jerk we were all glad to be rid of him. He wasn't even a member, you know. He wasted all his money on gambling. I just couldn't take it anymore. The only problem the kids had was when I remarried and they had to start taking orders from a man they'd never seen before. I guess you know what it's like having a step-parent."

Unfortunately. Although I'd gotten along well enough with Dean, I always had to hide my true feelings about his mother. After my mom died in a car accident three years ago, I'd expected my father to marry again. After all, he was only forty-five. But when he brought Louise home last October and announced a day later that they were engaged, I was shocked.

I'd hoped at least to get a chance to know her first, but even Dad didn't get that chance. Nine weeks after he met her, they were married. She moved in and threw out half of my mom's things while I was at school one day, without even offering to let me have any of them. Then she changed the drapes, the carpet, rearranged the furniture, changed everything around in the kitchen, and made me feel like an outcast in my own home I'd lived in all my life.

She even wanted to rearrange my room and hinted almost every day when my father wasn't around that I was old enough to move out and should do so. That last may have been true, of course, but was really between my father and me. He'd told me I could stay at home until I graduated from college, and that was still one semester away.

"They all get along fine now," Wanda continued. "How about you and Louise?"

"Oh, fine." Really, though, she always managed to find something wrong with the way I dressed, or the way I washed the dishes, or the way I did anything.

"You'll like this," she'd say, placing a dessert on the table. "It has a lot of sugar." I was all of five pounds overweight.

Or she'd ask me to help clean the garage of one of her friends, on the day she knew I was going to the library to work on a paper. "Oh, I guess not," she'd say as if to herself, before giving me a chance to reply. "That would require work, wouldn't it?"

She'd even say things like that to my dad. "Oh, you'll like this movie, dear. It doesn't require any thought." Then she'd laugh to pretend she was joking.

I was impressed that my high school graduate father hadn't been intimidated by marrying a woman with a PhD, but I did wonder why she'd married him. She'd quit work immediately, saying she finally had a chance to be a full-time mother as the Church encouraged. I certainly didn't notice her spending lots of time on Dean, though. She seemed to prefer planning parties, complaining that my dad wasn't very sociable when he quickly grew tired of them.

I was glad that Mom and Dad had always gotten along well. They'd been married for twenty-six years, and I never heard them so much as raise their voices to each other. Mom went to Dad's tractor pulls to support him, though they bored her out of her mind, and he took her on a date once a week, usually out to eat, which my father felt was an extravagance but which Mom loved.

Once every couple of months, Dad would take her to a movie, though only twice in my life had I ever heard him say he enjoyed a movie. The first was *True Grit* and the second *Foul Play*. But he patiently sat through every Elvis Presley movie ever made. What he preferred, and what my mom liked as well, was to take off to the Smokey Mountains for a few days.

I never heard them say they loved each other, but there was an awful lot to be said simply for the absence of bickering. It was nice to see that a good marriage was at least possible. It would probably get a four rating, I thought, smiling as I glanced down at my computer. It made me believe a five could be achieved with a little more work, and maybe a little luck.

"I guess Brother and Sister Martin are glad to be going to the temple," I said. "How long have they been members now?"

"Over a year," Wanda replied. "I think a temple marriage is so much nicer than a normal one. I don't even like to think of my marriage to Rob. Of course, my wedding to Michael was probably nicer because I didn't have morning sickness at the time." She laughed.

"Probably so."

"Is that it?" asked Wanda, pointing off to the right.

"Yeah." I quickly scribbled down all the information I could as we approached the outlet. A Time Saver. Supplied by Amoco. Good. That meant a contract dealer, and it was one question less I'd have to ask in my interview. Two curb cuts on the primary street. Prices posted. Hours posted. Convenience food, of course. And yes, they had electronic pumps. I got out of the car, checked off the number of pumps and nozzles, and walked into the store.

As I waited in line behind the other customers, I noticed a *Star* newspaper near the check-out. "Liz to Marry Eighth Time!" "Madonna's Secret Lovers!"

Oh, please. Didn't people have anything more important to concern themselves with than worrying about other people's love lives?

Three more people got in line, so I stepped out and went to the back of the last person because we weren't supposed to make the employees mad by disturbing their paying customers. I smiled, knowing Wanda was probably already getting impatient. I'd been acquainted with her for eight years, and she was certainly a lot nicer now than she used to be before her divorce.

This was the first time I'd ever worked with her directly, though. She was on Church welfare, so the Bishop had helped her get this two-week job. I was saving up to go to Austria to get married, so the Bishop told me about the job as well.

In return, I donated two days' labor at the Bishop's storehouse in Slidell, filling food orders for poorer members of the Church who needed help. I wasn't required to work at the storehouse, but it was fun, and I felt I ought to give as well as take. Kind of like Mom and Dad did in their marriage.

I knew that in my own marriage, it would probably be harder. When Wiltrude had come to visit for two months last year, I'd planned to take her on a swamp tour, wanting her to get a feel for my home. She'd refused, saying she was afraid to see a snake, and she'd been mad when I asked if I could go alone, telling her it was something I'd long wanted to do, and my dad's friend offering the free tour might not offer again.

I was mystified she would be upset over this, but she said we only had two months together and shouldn't spend it apart. She was usually so reasonable that her anger worried me for what it might mean for the future. Was it really possible to get along always with anyone, even someone you liked?

I sighed as the line moved ahead slowly. The man at the counter now was buying a six-pack of Coors. I wondered if his wife minded his drinking. Or was the beer for her and not him?

I remembered when Louise left, she took me aside and said, "I know this is hard for you, but you need to know the reason your father is kicking me out is because he's an alcoholic and I've been trying to get him into rehabilitation."

I tried to look serious so she'd feel she scored a point, but all I could think was that Dad had never missed a day at work, and he always looked sober at home. We'd been Mormons for thirteen years, and he'd never drunk even before we joined the Church.

There were two beers in the fridge after Louise left, but they were still sitting there. I was sure she'd put them there in the first place, to worry me, which it did, slightly. If I could have a secret like being gay, my dad could have one like being an alcoholic. But every day when I looked in the fridge, the two beers were still there.

When I went home today, I expected I'd still find them in the fridge. I hoped I'd also find when I got home a reply from one of the schools in Austria to which I'd sent job applications. I'd be graduating from the University of New Orleans in a few months and hoped to teach English in Austria.

Wiltrude's parents weren't pleased at first with the idea of her marrying a foreigner, but when they discovered two months ago that Wiltrude's sister was dating an Ethiopian member in Vienna, she said I suddenly looked a lot better to them, though we were both happy they slowly seemed to be adapting to her sister's choice as well.

I couldn't help but wonder if Wiltrude and I would be able to stay together. We were going to be married in the Mormon temple in Bern, Switzerland. Marriages in temples weren't "till death do you part," but were to last for all eternity. But Dad and Louise had been married in the Atlanta temple, hadn't they?

Another man stepped in line behind me. Forget it. The interview wasn't that important. My supervisor had told me not to waste too much time if I couldn't get any information. There had to be priorities in this work. I'd guess at what I didn't know. I stepped out of the line and walked back to the car.

"Good interview?" Wanda asked when I sat down.

"Didn't find out anything."

"After all this time?" She sighed in frustration. "Shit!"

I smiled, thinking again of Wiltrude. No matter how surprised she was by something or how maddening someone might be, she never even said "Mist!" or "Verflixt!" equivalent to our "darn" and "drat."

She certainly never said "scheißdreck." She felt she should be in control of her emotions. One of the first things I'd observed about her was her sincere smile when faced with rejection by other people, which happened to us hourly as missionaries.

I'd seen her calmly wipe the saliva off her face after a woman had spit on her. She'd then gone over to a

Schreibwarenladen, bought a card, gone a few doors down to a different shop to buy stamps, and mailed the card to herself. Then she'd resumed her work.

I'd also noticed how she refused to talk negatively about one of her companions who we both knew had taken advantage of her. That was when I decided I needed to get to know her better. If she wouldn't criticize these people I felt she had every right to be angry with, maybe she wouldn't get too mad at me if I accidentally offended her. But it was curious that when I finally began considering marrying her, it was with the thought, "Well, if I *have* to get married..." Surely, she deserved better than that.

But I *did* have to get married. It was a commandment. Without a marriage, a successful marriage at that, I couldn't get to the highest degree of heaven to live with God. Even if I managed to be celibate, something praised by some other religions, as a Mormon I'd be condemned to a lower degree of heaven, which in essence was still hell since I'd be denied further progression.

And if I didn't marry, I knew I'd never be strong enough to be celibate. God only knew what kind of depravity I'd fall into then. Even now at school, I found myself watching the other male students, almost praying one would approach me. I needed a wife to protect me, but I also needed a wife I knew I could live with.

Fortunately, Wiltrude and I had been able to work together for over seven months, three in Graz and four in Vienna. Then a year after our missions were over, we'd spent another three weeks together in Salzburg, where I'd given her my mother's engagement ring on the banks of the Salzach

River, and then a week more in her home town of Innsbruck in the west, where she gave me a silver "promise" ring as we stood on her parents' balcony.

During her two-month visit to New Orleans the following year, she stayed in the room across the hall from mine. We lay on the sofa together to watch T.V., and I did enjoy feeling her warmth against me. We'd French kissed three times, and I'd even managed to get an erection once, which was promising. It had been over a year now since I'd seen her, and I was looking forward to getting back over there.

Our long distance romance was convenient in that I'd had a full-fledged relationship for years with only a couple of hours invested each week. In some ways, it seemed better than marriage itself. But we did need kids, and maybe sex with a woman, as unsatisfying as it was sure to be, would still be enough to keep me from thinking of men too much.

I'd decided right from the beginning I couldn't let Wiltrude know I was gay. I was afraid she'd feel unloved, and I didn't want that. Besides, it wasn't as if I'd ever actually had sex with another man. I was still a virgin, after all.

Opening my computer, I entered all the new information I'd managed to collect even with my wandering thoughts, and I guessed at the rest.

"How many nozzles did you count?" Wanda asked. Then she giggled. "God. The number of nozzles I've counted in my life. Michael makes how many?" She looked at me and laughed. "You have to be careful," she said. "You can't just pull up to a pump and pick any nozzle. You have to get one with the right kind of gas." She squealed and hit the dashboard. Then she picked up her scriptures while I continued on my computer.

The machine buzzed at me once for a mistake I made in saying liter instead of gallon, and I quickly corrected my entry. An hour later, we'd finished three more outlets. It was only 3:15, a half hour before we were supposed to stop for the day, but Wanda insisted we head back to base.

We were silent as we crossed the Mississippi River. Then there was some traffic on the high rise over the Industrial Canal, but before too long, we were at the La Quinta in New Orleans East, and after a brief explanation to my supervisor about why we'd come in early, I turned in my computer and maps and picked up two more packets of film and a handful of new survey sheets.

Then I was back in the car and Wanda was driving me home. She only lived a mile away from me in Kenner, and I was right on her way, so she picked me up and dropped me off every day. It saved me a tank or two of gas, and she was being paid for her mileage whereas I wouldn't be, since she was "the driver," so it worked out fine for both of us, though I still recognized it as a favor and appreciated it.

"Hope you get your fabric before the store closes," I said.

"Oh, I'll be there by 4:30, so I'll make it," she replied. "Then I'll sew all evening. What are you going to do?"

"The Single Adults are playing volleyball tonight."

"Sounds like fun."

"If Lynn remembers to bring her ball." I smiled, thinking of our sometimes disorganized meetings, and the disorganized people I had to work with. I hadn't expected the call to be in charge of all the Mormon Singles in the New Orleans area two years ago. The call had come from the bishop right after I'd announced my engagement and didn't consider myself single anymore.

Was he saying he didn't like my choice of Wiltrude? Or did he want me to be an example in showing everyone that getting married was better than staying single?

I'd heard some of the other singles say things like, "I'll be so happy when I finally get married," or "I'll sure be happy when I finish school," but it seemed to me we shouldn't put off being happy, that it was far too fleeting an emotion to risk postponing. If we couldn't be satisfied with ourselves now while we were alone, I didn't see how we could really expect to be happy later, either.

Instead, my thought was often, "I'm reasonably happy now, everything considered. I sure hope I'll still be as happy when I get married." All I knew was that my every "date" for the past couple of years consisted in ten minutes of reading Wiltrude's letter and an hour or so writing mine to her, and I had not felt terribly deprived of her company. I instead enjoyed reading and listening to music and taking walks and playing Scrabble and talking with friends. I enjoyed going wherever I wanted and staying as long as I liked.

I remembered in Vienna when Elder Hof and I had gone to visit a church member one evening for just a few minutes. But my companion had gotten caught up in the conversation, and even by 10:00, he wasn't ready to leave. The mission rule was bedtime at 10:30, so at 10:15, I suggested again it was time to go.

Even though I was senior companion, Elder Hof shrugged me off and kept talking. At 10:30, he still wasn't ready. At 10:50, I stood up and walked to the door. It took him another five minutes to decide to follow me. We didn't say a word all the way home.

The fact was, however, that this guy had been my favorite companion of them all. There wouldn't have been a problem even that night except that we were a "couple," and I couldn't leave when I wanted and just say, "See you tomorrow." The "couple" part put an awful lot of extra strain on our relationship, always having to decide on *everything* together.

And yet always having Elder Hof with me had been comforting as well. I never had to face any boring meeting, and creepy mission leader, any rude person alone. We shared the experience of getting chased down a stairwell by a man with a handgun. Rather than feel freaked out by the experience, as I may well have done if I was alone, we'd laughed when we reached safety. We shared the experience of peeing together off the roof of a nine-story building.

It wasn't a glorious experience, to be sure, but there was a certain intimacy involved that didn't happen in just a regular friendship. And we shared the experience of teaching a young couple only a few years older than us about the Church and then baptized the couple together. It did mean more to me because I did it with a companion I really liked.

I had looked on every companion as a marriage partner, trying to see if I could make our relationship work, thinking of the days when marriages had been arranged by others. As my mission progressed, I'd count them off, finding I'd been able to survive all of them. Every time now in church when I was called to work closely with someone, I viewed the relationship as a trial marriage to see if I could make it.

I'd survived all of these as well, but I wanted more than survival out of marriage. I'd had true success with Elder Hof, someone just thrust upon me by an arbitrary decision from our mission president. Surely, by choosing my own partner, I could make an even better success. Especially if that person had also had the experience of having missionary companions.

"I met my husband Michael at a Single Adults meeting," Wanda said, bringing me back. "We were married three months later. Which reminds me. Heard from your girlfriend recently?"

"Last Saturday."

"Y'all set a date yet?"

"Well, we've set the year."

Wanda laughed. "You better not put it off much longer. How old are you now, anyway?"

"Twenty-four." I decided against telling her that Wiltrude was three and a half years older than I was.

"I really don't approve of missionaries looking for a wife while they're on missions, but—"

"I wasn't looking," I replied, sighing, having heard this already from several other people. "I simply found her."

"But how can you get to know her without dating?" she persisted. "Y'all must have done more than you should have."

I laughed. I hadn't even masturbated more than a handful of times out there, even that being considered a serious sin. "We were just good friends on our missions. Isn't that what the basis of a relationship should be?"

Wanda was silent for a moment. Then she said, "But being in love is different. You need to be in love to get married."

"I don't know," I said. "I counseled several couples when I was a missionary. We weren't really supposed to, but sometimes when we were knocking on doors, people would just pull us in and start telling us all their problems. Most of them would mention how the 'magic' was gone and now there was nothing left."

"But it doesn't have to go away," Wanda insisted. "It'll stay if it's the right person. And if you don't have it at the beginning, then you *know* it's not right."

I considered for a moment and then shook my head. I masturbated all too frequently these days, always thinking of men, often of one incredibly attractive blond missionary serving in my congregation, though I felt rather proud that I'd managed never to fantasize about Elder Hof, even if I did occasionally still have wet dreams about him.

Sometimes when I masturbated, I'd pull out a picture of Wiltrude at the last second, trying to make an association between orgasm and her, but the trick usually left me feeling sick in addition to the guilt I usually experienced when just thinking of men.

"If being in love means swooning," I said, "or not being able to sleep because I keep thinking of her or not being able to be happy now while we're apart, then I guess I'm not in love."

And I hoped I never would be. After we were transferred away from each other, Elder Hof had been deeply depressed, writing me many letters saying how much he missed me, but because I was so afraid of falling in love with him, I'd *refused* to feel bad after he was gone.

I didn't want anyone, even a man, to have that kind of control over me. Because if anyone did ever have that kind of control, it would be a man, and I'd definitely be in trouble.

"Well, then why—"

"I can't think of another person I care for more deeply and want to spend my life with. She's my best friend, I miss being with her, and I'm glad we'll be back together again soon."

And it was mostly true. Though I was happy enough, I really had no close friends here, and I was afraid of becoming too content with what the Church said was only half a life.

There was a lot to be said for being single, but the longer I stayed unmarried, the more likely I was to become set in my ways and be unable to change or adapt as I needed to. I knew I couldn't make Wiltrude wait any longer than she already had without starting to worry about losing her. I only hoped I could stop wishing for nozzles and learn to be content with just the gas tank.

Wanda made a little noise in her throat but didn't say anything else. We both listened to the radio while we drove for another fifteen minutes to our exit. As we turned down West Esplanade and headed for my home, I wondered what I'd find. Had Louise taken more of her things off to her new apartment?

When she and my dad had argued in the last few months, she'd push him in the chest and scream, "Hit me! Hit me!" right in his face. I knew she'd worked with the Battered Women's Program before marrying my dad.

It seemed to me that someone who could be as sick and devious as to try to provoke a violent crime was capable of almost anything. Dad would always walk out of the house then, leaving Louise fuming. I wondered that if she'd come to get her things, if she'd taken some of ours, too. I stared at the canal alongside the road and let my mind go blank.

Wanda stopped in front of my house a few minutes later, dropped me off, and then waved as she continued on. I looked at the green lawn I'd mowed yesterday. It looked fresh and cool. The toilet paper was all gone. I walked to the back door and unlocked it, closing my eyes and breathing deeply.

Maybe my letter from Austria had come today. I stepped inside and closed the door behind me.

Tilly the Barbarian

"You seem like a real geek, Andrew," Ryker said, leaning over Andrew's desk at lunch. "Want to join me and my friends for a game of Heroquest tomorrow night?"

"Excuse me?" Andrew wasn't used to other people at work talking to him socially. Ryker had begun working here just a month ago, though, and had already made several attempts at conversation. Since Ryker wasn't Mormon, and smoked as well, Andrew had been polite but distant.

"Come on. You must know what people are saying about you," said Ryker, smiling pleasantly.

"Not really." Did people even notice him enough to include him in their gossip? It was a little flattering really.

"They say you're a social misfit," Ryker continued. "And I have three other misfits coming to my house tomorrow to participate in a role-playing game. We're all just weird enough that you might like us. What do you say?"

Andrew frowned. He'd seen Ryker's wedding ring, and a photo of a woman on the man's desk. He must not be gay, though from the little experience Andrew had, getting together to play games seemed a pretty gay thing to do.

Maybe geeks and gays were overlapping categories. Andrew was thirty, still single because he wasn't sure he could face an entire lifetime with a woman, but he was still a virgin as well, because he didn't want to face an eternity with demons and devils, either.

But life did get pretty lonely at times. Some days, he felt like a caveman trying to integrate into the modern world, always feeling out of place, never able to adapt as well as those cavemen in the Geico commercials on TV.

"Sure," Andrew said slowly. "It sounds like fun."

It really didn't. But what would it hurt to give it one simple try?

"Great. We usually start at 6:00 and go on until 10:00." Ryker gave Andrew the address. "It's pot luck. Can you bring some soda?"

"No problem." Andrew was already regretting his decision. Four hours? It seemed a bit much for a work night. But he was committed now, and he always kept his commitments, as any gentleman would do. He smiled, shook Ryker's hand, and then got back to work.

Throughout the rest of the day, he stole glances at Ryker, who was busily working at his own desk and ignoring Andrew. He checked the internet every once in a while for the latest news. A terrorist train bombing in Russia. A bomb in a Pakistani mosque. But no soldiers killed in Afghanistan today. Thank God for that.

It was Monday, so that night after dinner, Andrew headed over to Melanie's apartment for the Single Adult Family Home Evening at 7:00. Mormons, of course, devoted every Monday night to family activities, but since the Singles had no families, the Church grouped them together so they would both have a spiritual experience during the week and keep in mind that the ultimate goal was marriage and family.

Andrew enjoyed being with the others, though he was getting to be much older now than the core group in their early twenties. Then, too, the knowledge that he might forever be denied a family because of his condition was becoming more and more painful to bear. But like always, he smiled and pretended to have a good time.

"Did you hear what happened to Drena?" Melanie asked once the group was all gathered and had offered an opening prayer.

"What?" asked Scott. "I wondered why she wasn't here."

Melanie leaned forward and whispered loudly, "She's been disfellowshipped for petting with a guy from work."

Everyone gasped, and half the group laughed. "Well, she was always dressing inappropriately," Candace said.

"Why didn't she ever make out with *me*?" asked Ron, laughing.

"'Cause you didn't go on a mission."

"And her coworker did?"

The group continued bantering for several minutes before the lesson started, this one about the importance of reading the scriptures daily. Andrew felt vaguely uneasy about the gossip. They all loved Drena, obviously, but there still seemed to be something rather brutal about the talk.

After the lesson, they all played Charades for an hour, and then the group broke up and went their separate ways. Andrew arrived back at his place just after 9:30. Tonight's activities had lasted only two and a half hours, and he was still exhausted. He didn't know if he could handle the following evening. Maybe he should cancel.

"Andrew," Ryker said on Tuesday when he stopped by Andrew's desk during lunch. "About tonight."

Andrew smiled. Maybe he was being uninvited. Perhaps someone in Ryker's group was calling in sick.

"It looks like we really need a barbarian in our game. We already have a wizard and an elf and a dwarf. But if you agree to be a barbarian, you can be any race you choose."

Andrew frowned. "You mean, I can be Filipino?"

Ryker laughed, a beautiful, hearty laugh. "I mean you can be human or orc or a dwarf."

"Dwarves aren't human?"

Ryker laughed again. "You'll catch on before long. Why don't you start out as a human?"

Andrew nodded, and Ryker went on his way. Andrew felt like a monster most of the time because of his depravity. Maybe playing a human would help.

As long as he could avoid falling in love with Ryker. Andrew knew it was hopeless, that Ryker was straight, and that in any event, Andrew was committed to living a gospel-centered life. But he felt a tingle now as he remembered that laugh. He hoped he wasn't making a mistake.

Andrew picked up some diet root beer on his way to Ryker's house. It was a modest home in a working-class neighborhood. Andrew arrived at five minutes to 6:00. He hated being late. Tardiness was so crass.

"Buddy! Come on in!" Ryker greeted him at the door with a hug.

What was that all about?

"Andrew, this is my wife, Kelly. Kelly, this is my coworker, Andrew."

"I've heard so much about you."

Andrew laughed. "I seriously doubt it."

"Well…"

"Come on in the dining room. We'll get set up."

Andrew put his sodas on the kitchen counter and then joined Ryker around a large table covered with a tan tablecloth. There was a paper playing board set out, which simply contained a pattern of squares, and at the head of the table was a thin cardboard partition that said Overlord. Andrew hoped he wasn't getting into anything Satanic. There were lots of dice, and a handful of little plastic figurines.

A few minutes later, the doorbell rang and another man walked in without waiting for permission to enter. "Hey, Maddock. This is Andrew."

"Nice to meet you."

"You, too," said Andrew.

"Maddock's a wizard."

Andrew didn't know how to respond to that and finally managed, "How nice for you."

Maddock laughed. "You were right about this one, Ryker."

So they'd talked about him? Andrew felt his ears burn, but the guys didn't seem mean-spirited. If they didn't like him, why would they have invited him?

Perhaps he was here to provide jokes later after he was gone?

A moment later, another man walked in, more handsome than the others. Andrew suddenly felt nervous.

"Hey, Gavin. This is Andrew, the guy I was telling you about."

Gavin gave Andrew a surprisingly brazen appraisal. "Can I sit next to him?"

"No footsie under the table," Maddock warned.

Andrew's whole face was burning now. "Gavin's our token queer," Ryker explained. "And we thought he could use some company."

"What do you mean, company?" asked Andrew, trying not to stutter.

"Oh, don't worry. You don't have to sleep with him unless we do a Saturday evening session that goes on all night."

Andrew was mortified.

"So how are those baby plans coming along?" Maddock asked, thankfully allowing Andrew time to recover.

"The doctor says my vasectomy may be reversible," Ryker responded, "but if not, we may have to go in with a needle and extract some sperm."

"Ouch."

"How's Carol's pregnancy coming along?"

"The morning sickness is getting better."

Gavin nudged Andrew. "Breeders," he muttered, rolling his eyes.

Andrew didn't know what shocked him the most. The casual talk of heterosexual sex, the casual talk of homosexuality, or the casual acceptance that the straight men had for the gays.

Or the shock that his own orientation had been so apparent.

Teague showed up a couple of minutes later. Everyone was in their early to mid-thirties. Andrew instantly felt a new level of comfort despite all the audacious talk. And it was nice they were all guys, even if…well, Andrew didn't know if it was the gay man or the straight men who were more challenging to accept.

Just before the game began, there was another scandalous moment almost too great to bear. "What would you like to name your character?" Ryker asked.

Andrew hadn't thought about it. How much could he allow himself to play? Could he name his character Arnold after Schwarzenegger? He looked about at his fellow players. Even the humans in the room had more interesting names than Andrew did. He was just a boring, boring person.

"Ralph?" he asked, feeling downright stupid.

"No." Gavin shook his head. "Let's name him Tilly." The others all laughed, and Andrew's character was named for him. He was mortified at the effeminate name, and yet despite his burning ears, Andrew felt a little thrill as well. What would the Single Adults group think if they knew? The thought was funny at first but then quickly became sobering.

As the group looked for traps and treasure and fought zombies and other creatures, Andrew tried not to be shocked any further. But Maddock's male wizard was named Scarlet and spoke like a Southern belle, even though Maddock was supposedly straight. All the other players spoke in their character's voices, acting out entire scenarios at length. It struck Andrew as silly, and yet he envied the freedom these guys seemed to feel. They *luxuriated* in it.

The evening wore on, and Andrew found himself laughing at the jokes the others told. Maddock had blue balls because his wife was no longer interested in sex while pregnant. He joked about beating off while fantasizing about Ryker's wife. Then there was banter about Ryker not being a real man because of his vasectomy. But there was no cattiness, no meanness associated with the joking.

At the end of the game, Teague's dwarf was killed, and Maddock's wizard pulled a card which gave him an elixir of life to bring back one dead comrade. The elixir was a "pearly white liquid" to be applied to the character's face. Everyone howled, and even Andrew understood the implications.

"Straight men have all the fun," Gavin said wistfully.

"I don't know," said Teague. "You guys get to do this in real life."

The audacity, the depravity, the sinfulness, the baseness of such talk was shocking, but even these straight married men who weren't sinning at all in their sex lives were joking as if this were nothing.

Soon, too soon, the evening was over, and yet the surprises continued as all four men hugged Andrew good-bye. Mormons always shook hands, which Andrew loved, because non-members so often didn't have any physical contact at all, but these guys *hugged*. Were they really straight?

Maybe they'd done as he was contemplating, married women they weren't attracted to. But if they were this accepting of homosexuality, why would they have bothered? Was it simply that non-members didn't understand the gravity of the situation? Perhaps he should stay far away from them, after all.

Andrew went home, checked the news for the latest from Afghanistan, and read another chapter in the Book of Mormon. When he grew tired of that, he kneeled beside his bed. "Please don't let me be corrupted," he prayed wearily. He climbed into bed and smiled weakly, despite his worries. It had been a fun evening.

Ryker was friendly to Andrew at work, though their paths didn't directly cross very often throughout the day. He made a point of assuring Andrew the other players liked him and wanted him to return the following Tuesday. Andrew agreed, still unsure what was best.

Saturday night was a Singles dance at the stake center. Andrew went and asked a few of the less attractive girls to dance. They didn't look any more excited about it than he did.

Church on Sunday went as usual. It was Andrew's turn to teach the Elders Quorum lesson. He wasn't much of a teacher, going straight from the manual. The class naturally found it boring, but what was he to do? The bishop had called him to the position, and no matter how unqualified Andrew was, he had to do his duty. It would be uncivilized not to.

The only interesting part of the lesson came near the end, when Andrew stumbled over part of the material, and there was a long moment of silence. Tony, the second counselor in the Elders Quorum, took the opportunity to make an unrelated comment. "Hey, did everyone hear what's going on in Uganda?"

"No."

"What?"

"They're proposing a new law that will sentence gays to death. And anyone who knows of a gay person will get three years in prison if they don't report that person to the authorities."

"All right!"

"About time."

"Doesn't that seem too extreme?" This comment came from Edward, who was married with two kids.

"These guys are trying to destroy marriage. They'll take us back to the Stone Age."

"There were gays in the Stone Age?"

"You know what I mean. Gays want to destroy civilization."

"Well, maybe if the law passes, and other countries don't protest, the world will see that no one cares, and other places can follow suit."

"Homosexuals just want to reduce us to animals."

"There are gay animals?" Andrew asked, biting his lip for joining in the discussion when he still had other points the manual wanted him to make.

"All I'm saying is we ought to consider harsher penalties in this country. You saw the latest poll? Utah ranks lowest in the nation in attitudes toward gay rights."

"You have that backward. Utah is first in the nation in support of righteousness."

"The bottom line is that gays are trying to destroy the Church, and God will never allow it. He'll wipe them out one way or another."

The talk threatened to go on, but Andrew forced himself to clear his throat loudly. "*Anyway,*" he said, trying to regain control of the class, "the next point of the lesson, if you'll turn the page…"

The elders had clearly been more interested in this topical argument than in Andrew's lesson, but Andrew couldn't bear to hear the hatred in their voices. They'd cut him out of their lives in a heartbeat if they knew his secret. How could he ever feel the brotherhood of the Church, knowing these people despised him?

It wasn't theoretical. He could *hear* the loathing, *see* the disgust in their eyes.

It was like reading someone's email sent to you by mistake and learning they really hated you but had never said anything out loud before. You couldn't tell them you'd seen the email, and you had to keep interacting with them as if you didn't know the truth.

Andrew's mind wandered more than usual during Sunday School and Sacrament meeting. In some ways, the Church had grown more understanding toward homosexuality over the years. But as last year's Proposition 8 in California had proven, the Church and its members still hated gays, despite whatever "gentle" phrases they might try to use.

He was contaminating himself by playing with Ryker and his friends on Tuesday. The battle was hard enough when he was pure. He'd never manage it with an evil spell cast over him. And that's what the devil was doing by luring him there.

Andrew spent the rest of the day reading a book by Boyd K. Packer and then watching *The Other Side of Heaven*. He felt better by the time he went to bed.

Andrew determined the next day to tell Ryker he couldn't make the Tuesday night meeting, yet somehow, they never seemed to run into each other all day, and Andrew was left with the commitment to say something first thing the following morning.

Monday night was Family Home Evening again at Melanie's apartment. Drena was there this time, and everyone acted happy to see her. She was frank about her recent troubles, admitting to spending the night with her boyfriend. "But we broke up," she said. "I guess I kind of provoked it, in order to save my character."

"What did you do?" asked Candace.

"Well, he had this horrible monkey. It was always masturbating."

Everyone laughed nervously.

"And it threw feces all the time."

"Ugh."

"He had it in the back yard in its cage during the daytime last Saturday. But he forgot to bring it in at night because he was distracted by my sleeping over. *I* remembered the monkey, but I hated it, so I left it outside. And of course, you remember how cold it got last weekend." She shrugged. "The monkey was dead by morning."

There were a couple of gasps, followed by laughter. Andrew, though, was appalled. Drena had killed a living creature just to break up with her boyfriend? Even if she'd done it simply out of hatred for the animal itself, nothing seemed an adequate justification. How could everyone be laughing about it like it was merely a naughty prank?

The group settled down shortly and they shared a lesson on the importance of prayer. Then they played Pictionary, and everyone went home.

Andrew lay in bed a long while, thinking.

The next morning when his alarm went off, Andrew thought about calling in sick to work. But that wouldn't be right, so he got dressed and ate a quick breakfast. He avoided Ryker for most of the morning, but during lunch, Ryker stopped by Andrew's desk.

"How's Tilly doing?"

"Oh, uh, um, just fine."

"So we're still on for tonight?"

"Sure."

"Great. Gavin will be pleased."

With that, Ryker left, and Andrew had to figure out what he meant by the comment. Was Gavin interested in him? Should Andrew change his mind and cancel in order to protect himself from temptation? Perhaps Gavin simply liked not being the lone gay man in attendance.

Andrew knew what it was like to be all alone. He always felt like a loathsome bug at church. But maybe Gavin just liked him as a friend. It would be nice to have a real friend, wouldn't it?

Someone you could be around without a mask, without your armor.

There wasn't time to worry about it too much, though. There was plenty of work to do, and Andrew barely had time to check Yahoo for news just once around 4:00. There was a mass shooting in Michigan, and a reference to the fact that Utah was the only state that allowed guns on school campuses. Two soldiers were killed in a helicopter crash in Afghanistan. Andrew's heart skipped a beat, as it did every time he heard bad news from the region. He hoped that Steven was okay.

Andrew barely even knew Steven. The man was seven years younger than he was. Andrew had sent him a couple of encouraging letters when Steven was a missionary in Sweden. It wasn't till he came home, looking like a real man for the first time, that Andrew had really sat up straight to take a good look. He tried to befriend the young man in the Single Adults program but not two months after he returned to the States, Steven had joined the Army, and now he was stationed in Afghanistan, fighting the evil Taliban.

Part of Andrew admired Steven for it. But part of him hated that the man was forced to live in the desert in a Third World country where the literacy rate was only 10%. Part of him felt that unchecked, terrorists could precipitate World War III. But part of him also felt that aggression on our part was only exacerbating the problem.

Why did people like to fight so much anyway? Why did grown men like Ryker and Gavin think *pretending* to fight every Tuesday was a fun pastime? It almost seemed insulting to be playing a game of pretend heroism while Steven was facing bullets and roadside bombs every day. Maybe tonight should be Andrew's last time.

Andrew brought cans of diet crème soda tonight, and shortly after 6:00, the gang was all seated, ready to play. "The doctor *is* going to have to use a needle to get my sperm," Ryker announced.

"Barbaric," muttered Teague.

"What's barbaric is living with a pregnant wife," Maddock said, putting his hand to his forehead. "I wish some of these spells in my bag were real."

"That's advanced gaming," said Ryker. "We're not ready for that yet."

Everyone laughed except Andrew, who was afraid again he was getting in over his head with some kind of witchcraft. "Look, guys, I'm Mormon," he said abruptly, his heart beating hard. "I don't know if I feel comfortable playing."

"You're Mormon?" Gavin asked. "Hey, did I ever tell you guys about when I took a tour of the Mormon temple here before they opened it? Apparently, heathens are only allowed to see the place before it's 'dedicated,' and then only card-carrying Mormons can go in after that. Is that right, Andrew?"

Andrew nodded uncertainly.

"Anyway, I went in with all these stickers that said, 'Gay Christians have met here,' and I put them everywhere. I put them underneath vases, under chairs and sofas, inside drawers, underneath toilet lids, absolutely every place I could think of."

Andrew's mouth fell open in horror.

"Then when I got home, I called the temple and told them what I'd done. I said I'd placed one hundred stickers, but I really only placed ninety-one. I figured they'd tear the place up looking for those last nine."

Everyone howled, and as horrifying as the story was, Andrew found himself slightly impressed.

"Speaking of barbaric, they said what I'd done was vicious vandalism, and they threatened to prosecute me. But the temple was dedicated on schedule, and the world didn't seem to come to an end."

"It was a lot like after Prop 8," Ryker said. "The Mormons went on and on about all the 'violence' they suffered, which amounted to a couple of cans of spray paint."

"But…but…" Andrew spluttered.

"I understand," Gavin said softly. "I read Patty Hearst's autobiography. I know how brain washing can turn even a respectable person into a criminal."

Andrew's mouth fell open again. Had Gavin really said such an outrageous thing?

Of course, he completely disapproved of what Gavin had done, and yet as a brutal act, it hardly compared to what was going on in Uganda. Andrew had been reading the Church website and following the news. No major religious or political leaders in America had condemned the proposed law.

Inhumane.

Why wasn't the prophet denouncing it? The gospel was supposed to bring a civilizing influence upon the world. Was it just "not their problem"? The Church avoided speaking on "political" issues, but if gay marriage was a "moral" issue here in the U.S., then why wasn't the murder of gays a moral issue as well?

But tonight, instead of feeling like a worm, thinking about his position in the universe just made Andrew angry.

He behaved recklessly throughout the game, opening doors without checking for traps, being the first to engage monsters in battle, letting the others gather all the treasure. He felt he'd given up before even starting, and that made the game not as fun as it had been last week. And yet part of him enjoyed the recklessness, too.

"Andrew's really getting into this," Maddock said.

"If he gets hurt much more in battle," Gavin noted calmly, "he may need some special comforting later."

Teague laughed. "But you don't have any healing spells."

"I've got some pearly white liquid left over."

"Left over from what?" Ryker smiled.

"I beat off in your bathroom every Tuesday night, listening to your sexy voice through the door."

"Well, *I* beat off in your bathroom every Tuesday night, too," said Maddock, "listening to *Kelly's* voice through the door."

Andrew put his dice down and stood up.

"You okay?" asked Ryker.

Andrew was trembling. He knew this was a pivotal moment in his life, and he had to be strong. What he wanted was *everyone's* leftover sperm. But he was going to be good. He was going to be civilized. He was going to be a light set on a hill.

"I can't come here anymore."

There was only a brief moment of surprised silence before Gavin said, "We're compromising his virtue. I've seen it before."

"Is there a cure?" Maddock asked.

"Anyone got a spell?"

Ryker, who was sitting just to the right of Andrew, at the head of the table, stood up. "I don't know if I have any potions specifically designed to eradicate this problem, but I do have a magic wand." Without another word, he unzipped his pants and pulled out his penis.

There was immediate laughter around the table.

"Finally!" said Gavin. "I've been coming over here for ages waiting to see that."

This isn't consensual! Andrew screamed in his head.

"Well, I could live without the images I'll need to deal with when I go to sleep tonight," said Teague, "but…" He stood up and unzipped as well, pulling out his member.

Then Maddock and Gavin followed suit. Andrew watched in horror-struck fascination. The straight guys all had flaccid penises, but Gavin's was half-erect. What kind of friends would stand around doing such a thing? What kind of animals were they? The men were all pointing at each other and laughing, as if this were nothing, all except Gavin, who was just looking and smiling pleasantly.

"Come on, Andrew, your turn."

Andrew would *never* be so vulgar as to show his penis in public, and yet part of him sensed the camaraderie the others were feeling, and he desperately longed to experience such a thing. Part of him just wanted to be wild and dangerously lawless. And part of him wanted Gavin to see him and like what he saw.

He slowly unzipped and pulled out his fully erect penis.

"Not bad," Gavin said.

"Are you kidding?" said Maddock. "How can I possibly seduce Kelly now, seeing what I'm up against with *all* you guys?"

"Whose turn is it?" said Ryker. "Maddock, I think you're up." With that, everyone zipped their pants and got back to the game. Andrew sat down again as well, confused. He didn't want to leave anymore. They continued playing till 9:45. Then everyone hugged and Andrew drove home in silence.

It took him a long while to fall asleep.

Ryker stopped by during lunch the next day to say hi. Andrew brought his Book of Mormon to work for the rest of the week and read it during his breaks each day.

Saturday night was movie night with the Singles. They met at Melanie's for 8:00 to pop some popcorn and watch *The Rock*. "Nobody tell the bishop we're watching an R-rated movie," said Ron.

"Speaking of R ratings," Drena said, "did you hear about Steven?"

Andrew sat up straight and stared at her. "What?" Had he been hurt? Or—

"He got kicked out of the Army for being gay."

"No!"

"Really?"

The others laughed. "I always thought he was too prissy to carry a gun."

"Wasn't he nominated for Soldier of the Year? What a joke."

"He only joined so he could take showers with other guys."

"I wonder how many soldiers he's tried to rape? He's probably raping Afghani civilians, ruining our international relations."

Andrew stared at his friends in shock. They'd been praising Steven's patriotism just two weeks before. What kind of loyalty dissolved in mere seconds?

He nodded slowly. He'd always understood that Church members would abandon him without a thought, but to see that callousness in action was sobering. He felt as if he were watching some hulk of a man throw a tiny dog out the window of a speeding car onto a busy freeway.

"Steven is a good man," Andrew said softly but firmly.

The others stopped and looked at him.

"I never heard *him* gossiping maliciously," Andrew continued.

Candace turned up her nose. "Well, *he* can't throw stones because *he* lives in a glass house."

For some reason, the comment irritated Andrew. "And you live in a cave," he said coldly.

"Why are you defending Steven?" asked Ron. "Are you queer, too?"

Andrew stood up, walked to the bedroom to pick up his coat, and left without another word. Sitting in his car, he held onto the steering wheel tightly for several moments, thinking of defenseless Chihuahuas, which slowly morphed in his thoughts into mastiffs with spiked collars. Then he pulled out his cell phone and called Ryker.

"What's up, Buddy?"

"I was wondering if you had Gavin's phone number."

"Sure thing." There was no smugness or smirking tone to Ryker's voice, even though Andrew knew he must be able to connect the dots. Andrew thanked him and then took a deep breath, looking at the number in his hands.

"Hello?"

"Hi, Gavin. It's Andrew."

"Oh, hey, how are you?"

"Well, I'm thinking about next Tuesday."

"Yeah?"

"I decided my character needs a sword in addition to his axe. I'm in a fighting mood."

"What brought that on?"

"A surge of testosterone." Andrew wondered if it really did all come down to hormones. Was his spirit or his body in control? "Is there a sledgehammer in the arsenal?"

Gavin laughed. "I love my men butch."

"Can I come over to your place?"

Gavin laughed again. "Sure. I just showered to get ready for the bars later, but I'd rather see you."

Andrew smiled.

"And just FYI, I douched as well."

It took Andrew a moment to figure out what Gavin meant, and then he laughed despite himself. "I'll keep that in mind."

Andrew drove the few miles over to Gavin's place, following the directions Gavin had given him over the phone.

It wasn't hard to recognize the house when he arrived. There was a large two-story covered in Christmas lights, with lighted reindeer on the roof, and a large, lighted snowman in the yard.

That wasn't Gavin's house, though. His was the one-story beside it, dark except for the few strings of lights on the roof spelling out the word "DITTO" and an arrow pointing to the house next door.

Andrew smiled and walked up the front path. He paused a moment, thinking of Steven and whether he'd need a place to stay. Steven was certainly welcome to share Andrew's house if he wanted. It would be better, of course, if Steven's family still accepted him, but there was obviously no guarantee of that.

Andrew wondered how Steven's situation might affect his own future. Would he start dating Gavin tonight only to switch to Steven a few days later? It was so confusing not to have strict guidelines confining your every move. Even Heroquest had rules. But now Andrew had to make up his own as he went along.

He knocked, and a moment later, Gavin opened the door. He was wearing high leather boots, a tunic, and a flowing, hunter green cape. "Are you a weary traveler seeking lodging for the night?" Gavin asked in an officious tone.

"Uh, yes," Andrew managed.

"Well, we extend every civility to wanderers. Do come in." Gavin motioned for Andrew to enter, and he did so cautiously.

They stood looking at each other seriously for a moment, and then Gavin winked. "I thought we'd do some *real* role-playing tonight."

Andrew smiled, and Gavin grew serious again. "Our barmaid will serve you shortly, good sir, but first, let me show you to your quarters. Perhaps, for a small token of appreciation, I could arrange for you to be served in your room."

Andrew followed Gavin uncertainly, yet still smiling a little in anticipation. Gavin really was a misfit, it seemed, but he supposed he was one, too. Andrew realized with complete clarity now that he'd never fit into mainstream society. He wondered if he was starting an adventure tonight that would bring on battles against real ogres and giants, and if he was even starting out on level one, but he was willing to see where the story led.

Once in the bedroom, Gavin pretended to kneel down as the host of the inn for the purpose of removing Andrew's shoes. But that game ended pretty quickly as they moved on to a new one. It turned out that the douching did come in handy. Afterward, Andrew and Gavin lay on the bed cuddling. Andrew put his head on Gavin's chest, and Gavin caressed Andrew's arm lightly.

"This isn't a game, you know," Gavin said softly. "You of all people must know we have real enemies out there."

"Yes," Andrew replied slowly. "But we have the Overlord on our side, don't we?"

"Even with friendly overlords, elves get shot with arrows, and dwarves get their arms hacked off. Being gay isn't only about love. It's about violence, too."

Andrew was silent a moment. "You have any more of those stickers you brought to the temple?" he finally asked.

"Yes," Gavin replied in a confused tone. "Why?"

"I still have my temple recommend. I can get back in with them again next week."

Gavin laughed. "Barbarians aren't the best undercover agents, you know."

"The Mormons are the real infiltrators, though, aren't they?"

"You sure you're up to taking them on? Prophets are like wizards. They can cast spells over people."

Andrew reflected on the statement for a moment. "I may get killed in the first round," he said slowly, "but I won't go down without a fight."

"Well, I'm up for any kiss-ins you want to participate in." Gavin squeezed Andrew's shoulder and then touched it with his lips.

His kiss felt so civilizing.

"Sheesh, kiss-ins," Gavin continued. "You know, the real problem here is that our attacks are a lot less brutal than theirs. When you're heartless, you can fight pretty savagely."

"Then maybe a little more barbarity on our part is in order."

Just then, Andrew felt a bite on his nipple and jumped. A moment later, Gavin bit his other nipple, too.

"Animal," Andrew said, laughing.

"You have no idea, Tilly," Gavin replied.

But Andrew was pretty sure he wanted to find out, and to unleash the animal in himself, too.

"Call me Attila," he said and smiled. Then he bared his teeth as well.

The Mission President's Son

"We had a family that was all set for baptism," I said, "but it turns out the daughter knows you from school, and she said she'd never join any church you belonged to."

Josh, the mission president's son, stared at me in horror.

"I'm just joshing you," I said.

He clenched his fists and pretended to swing at me. "I *hate* when people use that word."

The truth was, we didn't have a family ready for baptism. We did have one investigator, a man named Carl, but I wasn't sure he'd make it into the font. But any investigator at all was worthy of notice. Normally, I wouldn't be able to go on splits with the mission president's son, given that he lived in Bellevue at the mission home and my district was in south Seattle.

But I'd convinced President Kincaid that the poverty in my area was more likely to be the kind of thing Josh would encounter when he left on his own mission in a few months. He'd just turned eighteen and graduated from high school, and as soon as President Kincaid finished his service, the family would be returning to Salt Lake. Josh would submit his papers from there.

My regular companion, Elder Rasmussen, was working this evening with another member, and they were using the member's car, so Josh and I were able to use our mission car. I drove up to the top of Beacon Hill and parked.

"Do you like tracting, Elder Bennett?" Josh asked.

"No one likes tracting," I replied.

"My dad said he enjoyed it on his mission."

"Yes, but your dad is weird. And look where saying things like that got him."

"The mission home is a lot nicer than our house in Salt Lake," Josh pointed out.

"Well, we won't do too much tracting tonight," I said, "but you need to get your feet wet."

"Just what I need. Athlete's foot. I've already got jock itch."

"Josh itch?" I said. "I get that sometimes, too."

We started knocking on doors. I did all the approaches. I remembered how excruciating it had been for me to attempt them as a greenie, and there was no reason to put Josh through that at this point. But it wasn't long before Josh began sighing more and more loudly as we went from house to house. Well over half the people who opened their doors didn't speak English.

Or at least pretended they didn't. Filipino, Vietnamese, Chinese, Ethiopian, and Latino residents would say something to us in their native language and then shut the door. White and black residents spoke in clear, plain English. "We're not interested."

After we finished both sides of a block, I turned to Josh. "Do you think you'd like to—"

"Yes, I'll do it."

I laughed. "You don't even know what I was about to ask."

"Doesn't matter. Anything is better than tracting. I'm going to tell my dad he's crazy."

It was going to be a long two years for Josh, I thought. I felt so bad for him at that moment I wanted to hug him. "Let's go see Carl," I said. We drove over to the Mt. Baker neighborhood where Carl lived in a basement apartment underneath his landlord, who owned the house. From the front yard, we could see the roof of a Lowe's building supply store. I knocked on the basement door and a moment later, Carl answered.

"Hi, Elder Bennett!" he said happily. "It's always good to see you. And who is this with you today?"

"I'm Josh. Just helping out for the evening."

"Well, come in, come in."

Carl sat in a small easy chair while Josh and I took the sofa. "Would you mind offering a prayer, Carl?" I asked. Carl gave a simple, quick prayer and then looked to us for our usual lesson. We'd finished all the missionary discussions by this point, so instead I read a passage from Mosiah.

"Any questions?" I asked when I was done.

Josh raised his hand. "I have one."

"Yes?"

Josh turned toward Carl. "Carl, I don't mean to be nosy, but are you gay? 'Cause if you are, you're going to have a helluva time at church."

Carl's face grew rigid, and I thought he was going to kick us out of the apartment. I of course knew Carl's story, but I hadn't told any of the regular membership about him. "I'm a man," Carl said stiffly. "I was born a man, I'm a man now, and I like women."

Josh looked at me and then at Carl and then at me again. "But that's not the whole story. I can tell."

"It's not important," I said.

"Oh, what's the use?" said Carl. He closed his eyes and sighed. Then he began wearily reciting what he must have been forced to explain far too many times. "My penis was badly damaged when I was circumcised as a baby, so my parents had the doctors cut off what was left, my testicles, too, and raised me as a girl. When I was a teenager, I got estrogen supplements and grew breasts. But I always felt like a boy. My parents finally told me the truth, and I had my breasts removed. I'm in the process of getting my penis back now."

Josh nodded. "So you're F to M."

"No. I'm M to F to M. It's not a sex change. It's a sex restoration. It's not the same thing in the least."

We talked a little longer, and then I had Josh give a closing prayer, and we headed back to the car. Once seated,

I waited to turn on the ignition. "Why did you ask so many personal questions back there, Josh?"

"Carl's a little effeminate. He's going to be miserable in church. Are you sure you want to baptize him? You're not doing him any favors."

I laughed. "The mission president keeps on my back all the time to get more baptisms, and the mission president's son is after me to get fewer."

"You didn't answer my question."

I looked at Josh. He could almost be my twin. We both were small and slim, with dark hair and olive complexions. Looking into his eyes was almost like looking into a mirror. I wondered if his chest had the same hair pattern as mine. I wanted to know if his ass was hairless, if his penis curved gently to the right. I wanted to dig my face into his armpit because…well, just because.

"I believe the Church is true," I said. "So I want everyone to be a member."

Josh turned away and looked out the window. "Some people are better off heathen."

All the next morning and afternoon, I kept thinking about Josh. When Elder Rasmussen and I stopped back at the apartment around 5:00, I said, "I think we should go on splits again. Let me see if Josh is available."

"And who will I get?"

"Another one of the stake missionaries."

"Ugh. They all think they're so smart because they've already completed their missions."

"Try to find something to do here that they could never have done on theirs," I suggested.

"Like what?"

I shrugged. "Go to Borrachini's Bakery and tract out the parking lot. Go to the light rail station and read aloud from the Book of Mormon."

"Blech. I'd rather have the stake missionaries keep acting superior."

I hadn't asked Josh about his availability tonight, but luckily he was free, so we went to pick him up again. Not only was he a nice change of pace from Elder Rasmussen, but the drive to Bellevue and back counted as Travel Time and reduced the number of hours we had available for proselytizing. Besides, driving was fun, and the long trip gave us an excuse to use extra miles we wouldn't be penalized for.

Josh and I headed for the International District, where we stopped at a fortune cookie factory. I wanted to ask how much it would cost to have Book of Mormon verses printed and inserted into a couple of hundred cookies. We could hand them out as treats when we tracted.

But the cost was more than our mission allowance made possible. So we drove over to the Sandrocks' house. They were a member family who had us over to eat every few weeks.

"We don't have any food for you tonight, Elders," Sister Sandrock said when she saw us at the door. "But we do have a problem for you."

"Sure. What can we do to help?"

Sister Sandrock invited us in, and we sat in the living room with her, Brother Sandrock, and their twelve-year-old son, Kent. "Kent's discovered masturbation," Sister Sandrock announced, "and we're trying to shame him into quitting."

"Mom!"

Brother Sandrock laughed.

"Sister Sandrock," I said, "I'd pick another battle if I were you." I looked at Josh, whose face had turned pink, not easy given his complexion. "And next time you're at the library, look up *Shaming Your Way to Successful Motherhood*."

"Oh!" She jumped up to grab a pen and paper. "Was that written by a Mormon? Sounds like something I could get from Deseret Book."

"Sister Sandrock," I said. "I'm just joshing you. There's no such book. And for a good reason."

Josh glared daggers at me, reaching over casually to pinch my arm.

"Ouch!"

After we left, Josh and I walked half a block back to our car. But I didn't turn on the ignition right away. "Josh, do you ever think about having kids?"

"I'm not sure I'm going to have any."

"Why not?"

He didn't answer, so I decided to change topics, hoping to bring it back around again later. I definitely wanted a son I could raise to have a better sense of what true masculinity meant. And a daughter I could teach to be strong enough to put up with all the men who didn't know.

"What do you want to be when you grow up?" I asked.

I wanted to be a meteorologist. I could hardly wait to start college. I'd had to leave on my mission a month after graduating high school.

"I'm already grown up.

"You didn't answer my question."

He stuck his tongue out at me. "Not a college professor, that's for sure."

"Why not?"

"My dad's always having nightmares about it. The other day, he dreamed he'd written out his lecture notes, but when he got up in front of the class, he couldn't understand his own penmanship. Everyone was waiting for him to talk, he was sweating bullets, and the sweat dripped on the paper and made it even harder to read. The students started raising their hands to ask him something, and he wanted to run out of the classroom, but his feet were glued to the floor."

"Sounds like he doesn't like teaching, either."

"No, he loves it. I have no idea why he has nightmares all the time."

"Any idea what *you* want to do?" I asked.

Josh turned away and looked out the window. "I don't care," he said. "I just want to be free."

"Nice job if you can get it."

Josh turned to face me. "Don't you ever think about…think about…?" I saw his eyes register my entire face, my eyes, my nose, the slight stubble on my chin, and my mouth. When I started to say something and my lips parted, he looked as if he was going to jump in.

I leaned over to him, my face hovering just inches from his. I looked at his lips while he looked at mine. I leaned forward another couple of inches and kissed him. He didn't pull away. "I want to be free, too," I whispered.

The following day was Preparation Day, and I invited Josh to join Elder Rasmussen and me at Sam Smith Park on top of I-90. Elders Morrison and Kimball came, too. While the others were playing Frisbee, I ran off toward the bathroom to urinate. Josh followed.

He stood at the urinal next to me, and it was all I could do to relax enough to pee. When I finished, Josh reached over and touched my penis. He hadn't needed to pee at all, but his penis was hanging out, too, and I reached back and touched his. Then we zipped up and went back to join the others.

The next day when I asked Elder Rasmussen if we could go on splits again, he shook his head. "You're giving me an inferiority complex," he said. "It feels like you don't want to be with me anymore."

"Of course I like you," I said. "It'll be just the two of us tonight."

All evening as we worked, I kept thinking about Josh's tender lips.

I didn't ask for splits the following day, and the day after that was Sunday. I wished I could at least attend the mission president's ward in Bellevue instead of our local south Seattle congregation. But I sat through Sacrament meeting and Sunday School and tried to learn spiritual truths to make myself a better person.

Walking through the lobby on my way to Elders Quorum, I saw Carl sitting on the sofa. He was crying like a woman. No one was trying to comfort him. There was an open area around him like bacteria in a Petri dish growing penicillin.

"What's wrong?" I asked. Elder Rasmussen looked too uncomfortable to stay and kept walking.

"Bishop Wright says I can't go to Priesthood meeting because I'm not a real man." He sniffed. "And he says I can't go to Relief Society because I'm not a real woman. I have to sit out here while you guys go to class."

I gritted my teeth, forced myself to relax, and sat down beside Carl on the sofa. I put my arm around his shoulders. "It's going to be okay," I said.

"I need another dose of testosterone." He sniffed. "Can you come by later and inject me?"

"Let's go right now. I'll get my companion and we'll head right over to your apartment."

We followed Carl home, Elder Rasmussen unusually silent the whole way. "I'll wait in the car," he said. This was a major breach of mission etiquette. When I gave him a look, he only said, "I don't want to see another man's ass." I rolled my eyes and climbed out of the car.

Inside, Carl explained how to give him the injection so I wouldn't hit any major nerves. I aimed, took a deep breath, and jabbed the needle in his behind, slowly pressing on the plunger because the liquid was so thick. Then I pulled out and stood up.

"Thanks, Elder Bennett." He paused. "Too bad Josh isn't your regular companion, isn't it?"

"What do you mean?"

Carl smiled and led me back to the door.

Sunday night, Elder Bennett and I had dinner with a member family, and Monday morning, we tried talking to people on the street. It went as well as usual, which is to say, it was completely unproductive. That evening, I brought up the topic of splits again. "Oh, all right, Elder," my companion agreed. "At least this way you can visit Carl without me."

We went to pick up Josh, and then I dropped Elder Rasmussen off at another member's house so they could pair up for the evening. But Josh and I didn't head for Carl's apartment as we'd planned. Instead, I drove us to Seward Park on the edge of Lake Washington. It was still light out, and we took a walk along the outer edge of the park.

"I've been thinking a lot about you," I said.

"And you know I've been thinking about you, too."

"Good things, I hope?"

Josh kicked at a small branch on the asphalt pathway. "I wish I were your real companion." He paused, and I remembered what Carl had said. We really should be visiting him tonight. Analyze what the Proclamation on the Family said about gender. Show him that his wanting to be a man was actually exactly in line with Church teachings and that Bishop Wright was just a prick. "I think about it all the time."

"Not just at bedtime?" I said with a smile.

"Elder Bennett!"

"I know, I know. Yes, I want to be with you while you do sit-ups, and while you study your math homework, and while you watch TV. I want to be with you all the time, too." I paused. "But especially at bedtime."

We walked along in silence a while longer. "We're leaving in a couple of months," Josh said, "and my father will probably transfer you before then. I may never see you again."

"I'm going back to Salt Lake like you are. Are you going to serve a mission?"

"I don't know. But probably. I think I'd like to go to Germany or Switzerland or Romania. How else am I ever going to go someplace like that?" He paused to pick up another small branch and flung it as far as he could into the lake. "Besides, I really believe the Church is true."

"Yes," I said sadly, "so do I."

We kept walking around and around the perimeter of the park until it grew dark. Then we headed back for the car. We sat there holding hands in silence as the other cars in the area eventually drove off once the park was closed. "I love you," Josh whispered, giving my hand a squeeze.

"You're not just joshing me, are you?"

"I'm gonna slug you."

I laughed. "I have a better idea. Why don't we get in the back seat and make out?"

"Really?"

I opened my door and then crawled into the back of the car. Josh did likewise. We sat there trembling as we looked at each other, and then I leaned forward and kissed him again. This time, we used our tongues, and the kiss didn't end for a long time. We scooted closer to each other on the seat, and Josh began untying my tie. I unbuttoned his shirt.

Before long, we were naked, with me face down on the back seat and Josh awkwardly trying to enter me without breaking my ribs or smothering me. When he was finished, he looked at my still erect penis and said, "I don't know that I'm up to sucking that now. I've never done it before. Why don't you enter me this time?"

And so we reversed positions and I forced my way inside him. All I had was a little Carmex lip balm to help us out. But we were determined and finally achieved success.

"Will you wait for me?" Josh asked after we returned to the front seat of the car.

"Two years will give me time to concentrate on my studies," I replied. "I still have a few months left, anyway. And I'll work out some, too, get in better shape for you."

"You look just fine the way you are."

"I'll find an apartment near the University of Utah," I said. "You can move in when you get back from your mission."

"Will we tell our kids how we met?" Josh asked with a smile.

"Let's worry about that when the time comes."

"I like trying to get pregnant," he returned. "I want to try again and again."

I waited till Wednesday to suggest going on splits again, and Elder Rasmussen didn't put up any fuss. Josh and I drove over to Carl's apartment and knocked. The lights were on, but no one answered. We waited a bit and tried again, but he apparently wasn't home.

Josh and I kissed but didn't have sex again. "I want to be sure we like each other for our company first," I said.

On P-Day, the elders decided to go to Sam Smith Park again to play more Frisbee. I called Josh to invite him, but he said he couldn't make it. I was worried I'd offended him the last time we were together. When I suggested splits on Friday night, he opted out again. I was afraid to ask on Saturday.

On Sunday, I discovered that Carl had committed suicide on Tuesday. The bishop knew, the Elders Quorum president knew, the Relief Society president knew. Everyone seemed to know but me.

After services, I called Josh. "Yes, I heard," he said softly. "The day after we had thought to go visit him but instead…"

I tasted bile and swallowed.

"I decided to go on strike. No splits, no church, and there will definitely be no mission now." He paused, his voice catching. "Even if it's all true, it's just too mean to be a part of any longer."

"Have you told your parents yet?"

"I may be bold," he said with a short laugh, "but I'm not brave. That part's going to take a while."

"You'll be back in Salt Lake soon," I said, "talking to your bishop about submitting your papers."

"But going back home twill be such an ordeal for everyone anyway," he said. "I might be able to slip through the cracks."

"Maybe I'll go home early," I said. "Find that apartment and get ready for you so you'll have a place to stay if your parents freak out." It sounded good, but I didn't think I could bear to leave even one day early if it meant not seeing Josh while he was still in Seattle.

"My dad's a good man. You can't complain about him."

"Yes, I can," I said. "I don't want my kvetching skills to get rusty."

Josh laughed sadly, but he was certainly right. I'd heard horror stories about other mission presidents and had to agree with him about his father. But even good people often acted irrationally when their kids came out as gay. I had no idea how my own parents were going to react, though I'd been dropping hints in every email, making up stories about gay investigators I didn't actually have.

"Just know that no matter what, I love you." I blew a kiss into the phone and hung up.

On Monday, I asked Elder Rasmussen if we could go on splits, and he refused. On Tuesday, Elder Rasmussen sat me down during dinner. "I asked President Kincaid to send you to Puyallup or somewhere far away on the next transfer."

"Why?" I asked. "Just because I like going on splits doesn't mean I don't like you. I didn't mean to hurt your feelings."

Elder Rasmussen gave me a long, steely look. "You need to get away from Josh. But don't worry. I told the president you were flirting with some of the member girls. I didn't want to cause him any grief."

"Elder…"

"I'm just trying to protect you," he said.

I felt suddenly trapped, suffocated, bound by leather straps. I wanted to run out of the apartment and all the way across the floating bridge to Bellevue. I wanted to phone, to email, to find Josh and hug him as tightly as I could. I wanted to try making a baby again.

I only had a few months left, but that was too many. I needed to get to Salt Lake and find an apartment. But I still needed time to prepare for my own homecoming.

"Thank you, Elder Rasmussen," I said. "You're a good man."

"I took your phone and deleted the mission president's number. If you need to contact the mission home, you'll do it through me."

I thought of my first kiss with Josh only a few days ago, our evening at Seward Park, our talk of love. I thought of Carl's misery and Josh's decision to go on strike. It didn't matter where I was stationed the remaining months of my mission. I knew I'd never knock on another door again. I'd keep dropping hints in my emails home to make my coming out as easy on my folks as possible.

And I tried to think just how I was going to earn enough money to take Josh to Bucharest on our honeymoon.

Bi the Wayside

"Out of my way, Elder Quinn," I said, jumping up from the sofa and running toward the bathroom. I shut the door and sat down, a gush of water flowing out of my bowels. This colonoscopy prep was harrowing. After the first two bowel movements, everything that exited in the succeeding fifteen trips to the bathroom was water, but I only had seconds between the time I sensed something happening inside and the need to be sitting safely on the toilet.

I had started fasting the night before, which would make it almost 45 hours by the time I was able to eat again. If I had to have this procedure done, I decided I might as well get in an extra petition to Heavenly Father. Especially since my companion and I finally had real investigators for the first time.

Walter and Jessica Tolman had listened to all our discussions, come to church twice, and were on the verge of accepting our baptismal challenge. One little fast might push them over the edge and into the font.

"Open a window, Elder Crandall," my companion shouted through the door. "I live here, too, you know."

"It's nothing but water," I replied. "There's no smell."

I came out of the bathroom a moment later, Elder Quinn eyeing me suspiciously. I waited another ten minutes and then drank another cup of the prep. The liquid was lemon flavored, so the taste itself wasn't a problem. The texture, though, was a bit slimy. It felt like I was drinking mucus, so despite the acceptable taste, I could barely down one cup at a time. I had to finish three liters tonight and another liter tomorrow morning.

"At least we're getting a night off from proselytizing," said Elder Quinn. "Too bad you don't need a colonoscopy every week."

I hadn't fully understood the doctor's reasoning for the procedure in the first place. My only real symptoms were occasional brief abdominal pains that didn't appear associated with gas, but that hardly seemed alarming. Missionaries rarely saw a physician at all and then usually only for minor issues.

I'd gone in thinking I had blood in my stool but it had turned out the red coloring was due solely to having eaten a whole can of beets the night before. Real blood, I was told, would be black and tarry. Still, Dr. Behrens insisted I needed the colonoscopy and, frankly, I was intrigued to try it.

Plus, like my companion, I wanted some time off from missionary work. Even with two good investigators, that still left 95% of our time with nothing productive to do. I drank the last cup of tonight's allotment around 9:00 and was ready for bed by 10:30. I leaned over to pull the covers back.

"Stop sticking your butt out," said Elder Quinn. "With you in the bathroom every fifteen minutes, I can't stop thinking about your butt."

"That's the most romantic thing anyone's ever said to me," I replied, batting my eyes. Elder Quinn stuck out his tongue. We'd been together two months and become pretty good pals, mostly because we liked so many of the same things. We both got a thrill from jogging at 6:30 in the morning. We both enjoyed making—and eating—breakfast burritos.

And we both hated missionary work of almost any kind. We were only supposed to do four hours of community service a week, but we did twenty, counting it as missionary work on our stats. Some weeks we volunteered at a thrift store. Other times we worked at a food bank.

Sometimes, we weeded people's yards. Even backbreaking manual labor was preferable to tracting or doing street approaches. To be honest, even visiting inactive members was more tiresome than President Kincaid seemed to realize.

"Thinking about your ass," Elder Quinn said softly, "makes me think about Walter."

"I've been thinking about him, too."

"Do you think bisexuality is really a thing? Do you believe maybe he's just all out gay?"

I sat on my bed and looked over at my companion. "It's hard to tell. He seems so open about it. Why wouldn't he just be with a man if that's what he wanted? Besides, he said if we had sex with him, he'd give up men forever and be a good Mormon. He must have a good amount of desire for women if he's willing to do that."

Elder Quinn shook his head. "I don't know, Elder. That sounds like a trick of the Devil. He's just trying to bring us down with him."

My companion was probably right, but the odd thing was I hadn't been offended at the proposition. Jessica would be part of the foursome, too, and she was pretty hot, even if Walter didn't do much for me. My great-great-grandparents somewhere back in my history had been polygamists, so it was impossible to think that sex with more than one person was *always* a sin.

If this was the only way to get the first and probably only two baptisms of my mission, perhaps I needed to put myself on the line. Once the Tolmans were confirmed, the Holy Ghost could inspire them to repent completely, and their repentance would then absolve Elder Quinn and me from our own sins.

Really, though, it was hard not to suspect Walter's idea of polyamory was better than Joseph Smith's. With one husband, five wives, and fifteen children, there was only one breadwinner for the whole mass of dependents. But with one woman and three men, there'd be fewer children and more income.

I definitely wasn't attracted to Walter. Or to men in general. But missionary work was all about sacrifice, wasn't it? I could certainly do this to get two people in the baptismal font. Walter said I should consider it being "Gay for Pray."

The Last Days were desperate times.

"Let's sleep on it," I said. "I'm fasting about it, too, so I think whatever we decide will ultimately be the right decision."

"I'm glad you're my senior companion."

I laughed. "I love you, too, Elder."

"Aww, now you're making me think about your butt again."

"Sweet dreams, honey."

"You are so mean." But he was laughing, too.

I slept soundly, without any need to return to the bathroom, until morning when I had to finish the last liter of the slimy mucus. I'd deliberately scheduled the procedure for 1:00 so as to take up as much of the day as possible. We had a dinner appointment with the Tolmans at 6:00 but other than that should be able to relax without thinking about lessons or pamphlets the whole day. Elder Quinn drove the car assigned to us up to First Hill, and we parked in one of the Harborview parking lots.

Now that the moment of truth was approaching, I finally began to grow a little nervous. A Filipino nurse inserted an IV into my right hand, flushing it with a liquid that made me taste something metallic in my mouth. I lay on the hospital bed in my gown, feeling a bit vulnerable without my garments on. But even with the constant sting of the IV, this was so much better than teaching people about the Church.

The thought made me suddenly feel melancholy. It was clear I wasn't a good missionary, probably not even a good Mormon. Losing my virginity to Walter would probably have almost no effect on my exaltation in any event. Maybe it would be best if Heavenly Father let me die today during what would normally be a routine procedure. I sent up a brief plea into the hospital room ceiling.

A different nurse wheeled me through some wide doors and down the hall to another room with the number 3 over the door. "At least it's not OR 8," I said, but she didn't seem to get the *Coma* reference. A male nurse told me to get on my side, and I tried to position my hand so that it wouldn't fall and dislodge the IV if I fell asleep during the sedation.

"How out of it will I be?" I asked.

"As much or as little as you want to be."

"Why isn't life like that?" I said with a smile. Then I considered that maybe it was. I seemed to be sleeping my way through these two years, trying to pass the time in as unaware a state as I could. I looked up at the screen beside my bed where whatever the camera saw inside of me would be displayed. "I want to watch," I said.

"You like the view?" the nurse asked, chuckling.

"That remains to be seen."

"Hope you're cleaned out."

A young man in street clothes approached and introduced himself as Dr. Cheng. He explained the limitations and risks of the procedure, and then I closed my eyes to await the entry. I'd never so much as experienced the dreaded prostate exam, so this was the first time anything had ever entered instead of exited back there. I felt the manipulation of my anus, and to my relief, I realized that it wasn't at all uncomfortable and was in fact even a little bit pleasant.

I didn't feel anything inside my colon. Perhaps that was due to the sedation. But I seemed to be awake for most of the procedure, watching my colon on the screen. I continued to feel a little manipulation of my anus, and it continued to feel intriguing. I heard the doctor mumbling in the background. "His prep is a 9," he said, whatever that meant. "There's one," he said at another point, but I couldn't see what he was referring to.

Maybe I was more out of it than I realized. I watched more of the tunneling, a little disinterested. The whole thing was over in less than fifteen minutes. It was when I felt the scope come out that the idea first occurred to me.

Could *I* be bisexual myself? I certainly liked girls, but the idea of having a guy put his penis back there didn't terrify me. Now after the procedure, I wondered if it was possible to be fully straight but still want to have anal sex. Gay men didn't have any special nerve endings that straight guys didn't have. If it felt good to them, there was no reason I shouldn't experience the same sensory input they did.

"Good job," said Dr. Cheng. "One polyp, which we cut out and sent off for biopsy. A little unusual at your age, but then, that's probably why your doctor had you come in."

"Dr. Cheng?" I asked, smiling groggily at him.

"Yes?"

"I'll always remember my first time."

He laughed, and one of the nurses wheeled me into the recovery room. I was ready to leave within five minutes, but they had me wait a few more. I put my clothes on and met Elder Quinn in the waiting area. We walked back to the parking lot and climbed in the car.

"How was it?" Elder Quinn asked softly. "I mean…you know…"

"I can show you when we get home," I said. "It wasn't bad at all."

"Show me? Really? I mean…you know…"

We parked in front of our apartment and walked inside, Elder Quinn pulling back on my arm to keep me from walking at my normal speed. "They said you should take it easy for a while."

"I'm fine," I said but then reconsidered. "I mean, I don't think we should leave the apartment for a while or anything, but I'm not feeling too bad."

"That's good."

I looked at my companion and decided to go for it. "I meant what I said earlier."

He frowned.

"Take off your clothes and get on your side. I'll get some lotion and show you what it was like."

"I don't know, Elder."

"One of these days, you'll have to get a colonoscopy yourself," I said. "You don't want to worry about what it'll be like for the next thirty years. Let's get the mystery over with so it's not hanging over your head."

Elder Quinn continued to frown but finally nodded. We went in the bedroom, he undressed, and I grabbed a bottle of hand lotion from the bathroom. "I'm a little nervous," Elder Quinn whispered with his butt in my face.

"That's why we're doing this," I said, "to show you there's nothing to fear."

He let out a deep breath and I put a dab of lotion on my fingers. I pressed it against Elder Quinn's ass and rubbed lightly. He tensed up, but I kept rubbing gently until he relaxed. I added a little more lotion, rubbed again for a moment, and then inserted one finger gently into my companion's anus, just letting it enter maybe half an inch.

"Ooh."

He tensed again, but I moved the tip of my finger around very carefully, pressing against the sphincter softly. I didn't go in any deeper but just kept fingering the anus itself. "This is all it is," I said. "That's all there is to it."

"You're right," he said after a moment. "It's not that bad."

"Let me stay in a little longer," I suggested, "and it'll get even better." I continued to finger my companion for another minute, and then I pushed my finger in a little deeper. "To get the feel of the scope moving in and out, I'll have to move my finger a bit," I said. I started pulling my finger out and inserting it deeper again. "See? It's no big deal."

"Mmm. You're right, Elder Crandall. Thanks."

There was no way to justify staying in any longer, so I gently withdrew my hand and wiped the lotion off his anus with a washcloth. He sat up on the bed and looked at me. I wiped my finger off on the washcloth and looked back.

"I think we should do it," he said.

I smiled. "I think you're right. We'll tell the Tolmans at dinner tonight." I paused. "But we should get rid of the worry ahead of time, so we're not nervous when we see them."

I leaned over to kiss Elder Quinn. He started unbuttoning my shirt and then unbuckling my belt. I slid off my garments once more and turned my companion onto his stomach. Soon we were taking turns practicing full colonoscopies on each other. We put our scopes in again and again.

It was so much better without the IV.

Entering at the Rear of the Temple

"Do we have to keep coming to the temple every Preparation Day?" my companion asked wearily as we pulled into the parking lot beside several heavily waxed cars. Elder Gerard protested each time we did endowments for the dead.

"Don't you like getting out of the Rainier Valley?" I returned. Our district in south Seattle was rather dreary. We lived a few blocks from the huge, stadium-sized Goodwill on Dearborn, with a hillside of homeless tents under the bridge nearby. "Bellevue is so much prettier."

Of course, I wasn't here looking for beauty. I was seeking some kind of revelation from Heavenly Father about how to be more effective at missionary work. A mini-revelation about a new approach. I didn't need to see God in person. I just needed him to give me the germ of an idea. Nothing we were doing now was getting us anywhere. There *had* to be a way to reach the people in my area that I hadn't tried yet.

"We're not here to live in comfort, Elder Dorsey," my companion insisted. "We're here to bring souls to repentance."

I turned off the ignition. "And how's that working out for you?" I asked.

"Maybe if we didn't spend so much of our time endowing the dead…"

I laughed. "Are you telling me you'd rather spend P-Day proselytizing the living?"

Elder Gerard didn't answer.

"This'll only take a couple of hours," I said. "I'll treat you to an ice cream sandwich on the way home."

Elder Gerard was still frowning, but at least he nodded in resignation now.

We were discouraged from attending the temple every week, though I never fully understood the reason. Back in the Missionary Training Center, we'd been practically forced to go every week. Why the difference? I liked attending weekly for a couple of reasons. First, it made me feel like an adult with special knowledge, while so often when knocking on doors I felt like a stupid kid.

Probably because that's what most people yelled at us.

I also liked knowing I was helping those who'd lived on the Earth without having a proper chance to hear the gospel. But perhaps just as importantly, I wanted to finally feel the Spirit the way I was supposed to.

And maybe finally get that revelation.

I mean, I always felt *something* while I was in the temple. Walking down the hallways quietly in my slippers, the hush in the air was almost tangible. And the Celestial Room…it was impossible not to feel at least a little of the Spirit there, but I often felt I was only brushing up against the guy in passing, that we were never fully embracing. It was like trying to meet the popular girl at a party. She was always surrounded by other people, and I could never get close enough to say hi.

Elder Gerard and I swiped our temple recommends at the front desk to prove we were worthy enough to enter, and then we headed to the clothing rental counter. After our missions, we'd buy our own temple clothing and carry our own tiny suitcases like our parents did, but for now we rented.

"Do we really have enough money to keep coming here every week?" Elder Gerard whispered.

"You're getting a free ice cream sandwich out of this," I reminded him. "Stop being a whiny bas—" I stopped myself. "Think positively," I corrected myself. "You're gaining Celestial brownie points."

"Brownie points is right," my companion said. "You do realize where the term comes from, don't you? You're just kissing God's ass by coming here every week. You think Heavenly Father really needs his ass tended to?"

I thought for a moment, trying to think of a smart alecky reply. "I think he does," I finally said.

We changed into our white clothing in the locker room and carried our pack of accessories to the endowment room. It was 8:00 in the morning, and it looked like ours was going to be one of the busiest sessions of the day. Everyone wanted to check it off their list and get the task over with. Even I wanted the rest of my one day off for myself.

I wondered if the Spirit could be present among checklist saints.

Soon the lights dimmed, and the movie began. The creation of the world started to take shape, first flowers, then insects, and so forth. I gritted my teeth as the narrator talked about lions, and tigers, and—otters! Say otters!—bears. Elder Gerard pushed against me, and I realized he'd fallen asleep. I nudged him and he made a little "oh!" sound that let everyone around him know what had happened. Of course, half of them were falling asleep as well.

Finally, after another couple of hours, it was time to pass through the veil. I had the words and handshakes down pat by this point and entered quickly into the Celestial Room. There was a plush, light blue sofa I loved sitting on. Suede or felt or velvet, I couldn't tell. Elder Gerard looked as if he might deliberately sit on the far side of the room out of spite, but he eventually sat right next to me.

"Why do the dead need to hear the endowment session through our senses?" he whispered.

"What do you mean?"

"When we do baptisms for the dead, we do fifteen in a row. Dunk, dunk, dunk. Splash, splash, splash. The spirits don't need us to listen to all the missionary lessons first. They get all that information in Spirit Prison."

"Okay."

"So why can't the spirits get the endowment information up there, too? Why do we have to sit through that same boring movie over and over and over?" He paused and fingered his sash. "That *long*, boring movie."

"Be quiet," I whispered back. "How can I feel the Spirit in here with you babbling non-stop?"

I closed my eyes for a moment and tried to relax, hoping the Spirit might testify to me about that new missionary approach we so desperately needed. If I could come up with something truly special, I could pass it on to the mission president, maybe be marked for advancement. Moving up the mission hierarchy wasn't personally all that important to me, but doing so would prove I'd accomplished something useful. I prayed again for inspiration.

Heavenly Father, I implored, *how* can I reach more people? *What* do I need to do to touch their hearts? I wanted to feel their needs deep inside and help them.

It was such a struggle to feel special when every day we faced rejection after rejection after rejection. Occasionally, we'd run into a person with some type of mental illness or simply some sort of strange social maladaptation, and they'd miraculously be interested. Sometimes, folks like that even joined the Church.

But they either dropped away quickly or never really fit in. They were certainly not capable of moving into any leadership positions. Still, we were saving their souls, and that was something.

And as I had only baptized one single person so far, I'd be more than happy with another such weirdo on the books.

I looked about the room. People in white, wearing their green aprons and Pillsbury doughboy hats, were milling about quietly. It was the only time out of the multiple hours spent at the temple when we had a chance to reflect and pray, but I could already see temple workers coming over to usher us out.

No one was allowed to stay more than a few minutes. That was probably why people kept coming to do endowments over and over. It was the only way to accumulate any real length of time in the Celestial Room. It was like being exposed to radiation, only in this case we actually hoped for a cumulative effect.

Of course, other parts of the temple were special, too. I enjoyed walking up the stairwells rather than taking the elevator. The stairwells were always quiet and peaceful. And if I could get into an endowment room before everyone else started filing in, I could squeeze in a few minutes of peace then, too.

I wondered if there was a back entrance to the temple, some way to enter without being seen, some place to linger in peace just a few extra minutes. Some place where I could feel true, deep satisfaction at having connected in a primal way with another being.

"Look at those two people arguing," Elder Gerard whispered, pointing to an elderly couple on the far side of the room. We couldn't hear them, as they were only whispering to each other, but their arm movements clearly indicated they weren't happy. "Can we come back next week and do some temple divorces for the dead?" He smothered a laugh.

An elderly man in white walked over to us. "You should move on," he said quietly. I nodded and stood up. Elder Gerard followed me out into the hallway. As soon as we walked through the doors, whatever little part of the Holy Ghost I'd felt inside the Celestial Room slid out of my soul.

The pretty girl had been blocked off by other partygoers. The corridor was still quiet, with reverent people and thick carpet, but it just wasn't the same. Nice and soothing, perhaps, but I no longer felt receptive to the Spirit's probing. We walked back to the locker room and put our suits on again.

I wondered if the Celestial Room felt special merely because of the luxurious furnishings. The polished wood, the chandeliers, the flowers. Even in the lobby, I could feel *something*. The only other time I'd ever felt anything similar was when I was at an art museum on a low-attendance day. I could never feel anything special on high-attendance days. A person could only feel that special something when there was lots of space, lots of quiet, and hardly any people.

Was that why the temple workers shoved us out of the Celestial Room so quickly, I wondered? To keep it low-attendance? I remembered my uncle telling me about visiting the Sistine Chapel. The docents had to keep asking the mass of people to quiet down so they could feel the importance of the place.

I wanted to talk to the pretty girl at the party. But that meant I had to actually *be* at the party.

We drove back to our apartment in the Dearborn neighborhood, where I definitely did *not* feel the Spirit. Men trudged by in dirty clothing. Women cursed their young children. Trash fluttered by along the sidewalk in the wind. Broken signs advertised questionable businesses. A schizophrenic man yelled at a bus driver.

"Should we ask him the Golden Questions?" I asked my companion, pointing. He turned and glared back at me.

"That's Brother Shaffer," he said.

I looked again and realized he was right. Elder Rasmussen had baptized him last month. He was inactive already.

"Let's just go home and try to enjoy what little left we have of P-Day," Elder Gerard grumbled. We had to start working again at 5:00.

I pulled into the parking lot of a grungy convenience store and ran inside to buy two ice cream sandwiches. A bored Middle Eastern teen handed two shriveled chicken wings to an elderly black woman. Back at the car, I gave Elder Gerard his treat and he tore into it immediately. "Thanks," he muttered.

He was getting the slightest paunch, I noticed. I probably was, too. I had to buy him treats pretty regularly to convince him to try new approaches, but it looked like there was a price to pay. Perhaps we needed to find something more physical to do. Our bodies were temples, after all. We needed to keep them looking Celestial. I should have bought us both a piece of fruit at the open market instead.

"Why did Adam and Eve forget?" I asked, pulling back onto the road.

"Forget what?"

"They knew good from evil back in the Pre-Existence. We all did. So why did they forget?"

"They went through the Veil of Forgetfulness," Elder Gerard replied. "Like the rest of us. That's why no one remembers the Pre-Existence."

"But we know right from wrong," I said. "And *we* never ate of the fruit from the Tree of Knowledge of Good and Evil."

Elder Gerard took another bite of his sandwich. "We get it through Adam and Eve."

"But how? We're accountable for our own sins, not Adam and Eve's transgression," I said. "So why do we get the knowledge of good and evil from them? We don't get any other knowledge from them. We still don't remember the Pre-Existence."

"Well…"

"And what purpose did making them forget how to tell good from evil serve in the first place?"

"It was the only way they could transgress without sinning," my companion said. "And get kicked out of the Garden of Eden so we could all come here and get a physical body."

I pulled up to our apartment and we climbed out of the car. "Adam and Eve weren't perfect," I said. "Only Jesus was perfect. So at some point they'd have sinned and needed to be cast out of the Garden anyway."

"You think too much." Elder Gerard unlocked our front door.

"I guess we'll just have to go back to the temple next week so I can reflect on this in the Celestial Room," I said with a grin. *And maybe finally figure out that new approach.*

"You're killing me, Elder Dorsey," my companion said. "You're killing me."

We took off our suits as soon as we were back inside, and we cleaned the apartment in our garments, writing our emails home to our parents as the Hallelujah chorus played in the background. I made grilled cheese sandwiches for lunch, and Elder Gerard finally seemed to forgive me for this morning. I made another note to start doing something more physical.

"What are our plans this evening?" Elder Gerard asked while we got dressed again just before 5:00.

"I thought we'd stop people on the street and ask them about the Church. Maybe dance or something to get their attention."

Elder Gerard groaned. "That sounds like the absolute worst kind of missionary work," he said.

"What would you *like* to do?" Sometimes, it was easier to get cooperation if I let my junior make the plans, even if those plans were not one iota better than mine.

"Let's go to a porn store," he said.

I stared at him.

"The one on Dearborn."

"Are you trying to get us sent home?" I asked.

He laughed. "That's not a bad idea," he said. "When they wouldn't let Elder Merrill go home, he lied about hiring a prostitute and they shipped him right back. But I was thinking that a porn store would be a great place to call people to repentance."

"You don't think we'll be tempted to go inside and browse?"

"Of course we'll be tempted," my companion said. "That's why going there will get us extra points."

"Brownie points?"

Elder Gerard stuck out his tongue.

"Okay," I said with a shrug. Maybe the Lord was testing my humility. Perhaps the idea for a new approach would come through my junior companion.

The porn shop was close enough we could walk, but when we arrived and took up positions outside to try to talk to people, I put my hand on Elder Gerard's arm. "Let's take off our nametags and go inside," I suggested. If my companion was giving me the germ of an idea, I had to do whatever I could myself to develop it.

"What!" He looked as if he'd seen a temple patron wiping his nose on their apron.

Surprisingly, though, it didn't actually take much persuasion to get my companion to agree. We stepped inside the store and a friendly young man greeted us cheerily from behind a counter. I nodded back, and Elder Gerard and I moved over to a row of DVDs.

"Elder," he hissed, "these are gay movies."

At first, I could only see the images right in front of me, but I tried to calm down and take everything in. The store was large and quiet, almost reverent. I definitely felt something here, though clearly it wasn't the Spirit.

Yet it *almost* felt like the Spirit.

"You guys look new," the young man said, coming from around the counter to talk to us.

"Yes," I said.

"We have the DVDs and magazines up here," he explained, "the dildos and other toys back there." He pointed. "And the arcade over on this side." He pointed again.

"Arcade?" asked Elder Gerard.

"You know, the booths with the glory holes."

"Glory holes?" I asked.

The young man laughed and explained their purpose. "You guys better show me your IDs so I know you're old enough to be in here."

I fumbled with my wallet and revealed my driver's license to the man.

"Okay, well, have fun." The young man returned to his post behind the counter.

"We've got to leave right now," Elder Gerard hissed.

I held up a hand. "What's the one thing you've noticed about everyone who's come in so far?" I asked.

"That they're all a bunch of freaks!" Elder Gerard whispered back.

That was it exactly. These were weirdos, the exact kind of people we were usually able to interest in the Church. The *only* people we were able to interest. "I propose we try to get some referrals."

"Are you out of your mind?"

I looked about. Elder Gerard might be right again. This didn't look like the kind of place where people engaged in conversation. But what about the arcade? People had to talk through those glory holes, didn't they, to try to determine what they were going to do.

Or did people just stick their penis through the hole and wait? What if you wanted to suck? Maybe you stuck your tongue through the hole instead.

I looked at a man standing near us, fingering the DVDs. He was wearing a wedding band. That didn't mean anything, of course. He could be married to a man and not a woman. But I suspected there were a lot of closeted men here. Men cheating on their wives, if not physically, then clearly emotionally.

Men who would feel guilty and need to be absolved. Men who could be guilted into baptism to save themselves.

"Excuse me, sir," I said to the man. He looked at me as if I was crazy and disappeared into the arcade.

"What are you doing?" asked Elder Gerard.

"Finding us a Golden Contact."

"A Tarnished one, you mean?"

"*Any* contact is better than what we currently have."

Elder Gerard shrugged.

I looked at the DVDs and the magazines and the dildos and the arcade entrance. "I'm going in there." I pointed.

"Elder Dorsey!"

"You wait here by the DVDs. I'm going to find a contact. I'll be back in a few minutes." I took a deep breath and walked into the arcade. It was dark inside, so it took a moment for my eyes to adjust. There was a hallway with a series of doors on each side. Some of the doors had red lights shining above them. I picked a door without a shining light.

Inside, there was a video machine and a slot marked "Bills." I dug in my wallet and pulled out a one dollar bill. The machine took it and registered two minutes, which started clocking down immediately. I figured I'd need more time than that and put three more dollar bills in the slot.

There was a penis jutting through a hole in the partition dividing my booth from the one next to me. I put my hand on it and felt the hairs stand up on the back of my neck.

Was that the Spirit?

I kneeled down and pushed the penis back into the other booth. "Hey," I said through the hole. "Hey."

Part of another face appeared through the opening. "What do you want to do?" a man asked.

"I'm a Mormon missionary," I began, and the man laughed.

"You gotta be fucking kidding me."

"No, really," I said. "I propose we make an exchange."

"Of cum?"

"I suck your dick, and you let my companion and me come over and teach you."

The man laughed again.

"I'm serious," I said.

There was silence for a moment, and I wondered if the man was going to report me and have me kicked out of the store. I expected they probably had a "No Soliciting" policy here.

"Look," the man whispered back through the hole, "for something like that, I need more than a blow job."

"What do you have in mind?"

"You drop your pants and press your ass against the hole so I can fuck you. Then I'll let you come over and teach me." He laughed quietly. "And maybe we'll have a three-way at my place while my wife is out."

"No," I said. "This is on the level. We're not gay. We just want to teach you." I paused. "If you let me baptize you, though, I'll let you inside my back door as often as you like until I'm transferred to another area."

"You are one fucking weirdo." The man laughed.

I thought about green aprons in the temple. And secret handshakes through the veil. And pawing at the air like cats while chanting "O God, hear the words of my mouth."

"So that's a yes?" I asked.

"Sure," he said.

I stood up and turned around, unbuckling my belt and dropping both my pants and garment bottoms. I pulled my shirt and garment top up so the man would have free access to my ass. Then I backed up to the opening in the partition. I felt fingers putting something cold and wet on my asshole and tried not to jump.

A moment later, something big and fleshy pushed against my hole. I stood my ground and let him push it inside me. The man started pumping back and forth, rattling the partition wall. I grunted a few times but tried to endure it all stoically. After about six or seven minutes, he made one last, deep, painful thrust inside me and then pulled out.

I pulled my garments and pants back up and rebuckled my belt. I hurried out of the booth and opened the door of the other man's cubicle so I could get his address.

The booth was empty.

Well, I supposed some fornicators were liars, too. But at least I'd planted a seed. The next time the man came in contact with the missionaries, he was that much more likely to let them in. But I needed a referral tonight.

I was sure this new approach was the answer to my prayers. Meditating in the Celestial Room week after week while people roamed around in their temple robes and sashes had finally paid off. I spotted another booth with a red light above the door, and I went into the cubicle next to it.

I slipped a five dollar bill into the machine.

Then I kneeled down by the glory hole and whispered. "Hey," I said. "Hey."

P-Day Porn

Life is like a dildo. Intriguing. Appalling. Sometimes uncomfortable. Other times pleasurable. But always requiring careful clean up.

Kermit might have sung about how it wasn't easy being green, but he didn't know what real difficulty was. The life of a gay Mormon is *hard*. And not in a good way.

Let me share an example of the dildoish quality of gay Mormon life.

I had to sneak straight porno magazines into my missionary apartment so my companions could discover them and tell everyone what a horndog I was. The righteous elders in the district always looked down on me after the discovery, but I could see a glimmer of jealousy in their eyes as well. I was reprimanded harshly by my zone leaders again and again, but my goal was achieved—everyone thought I was straight.

That is, until the day my companion caught me staring at him from the shower as he urinated at the toilet.

"What do you think you're looking at, Elder Mortenson?" Elder Bigelow asked.

"A nice schlong," I responded. There was no point in lying.

"And why would you do a thing like that?" He'd finished urinating by this point but still hadn't put the damn thing away. He was shaking it a little, ostensibly to get the last couple of drops to fall off, but I felt like a fish watching a bobbing piece of bait on a hook.

"Because it's nicer than mine," I replied. "See?" I pulled the shower curtain farther back. Elder Bigelow looked at my flaccid penis with obvious disinterest. His attitude irritated me just a bit, so I stroked myself a minute, still staring at his penis. I was hard in five seconds.

"Oh," said Elder Bigelow. "I don't know if I can compete with *that*." He stroked himself a few moments and grew hard, too. "Looks like you're more of a grower and I'm more of a shower."

I laughed. "I want to be *both*!" He joined in the laughter, too. "Do you suppose that's what we get in the resurrection?" I was still stroking myself slowly. Elder Bigelow was as well.

"I don't know," he replied. "Do you suppose gods compare dick size?"

"Maybe," I said. "Don't you sometimes feel Heavenly Father is trying to prove something?"

"But wouldn't God have to travel to a different star system to see another god's dick? That's a long way to go to use a urinal."

I shrugged. "You're probably right. Besides, one god gets a hundred women. I would think it's the women who would feel compelled to compare genitalia, not the men."

"Damn, now you've got me hot and bothered." Elder Bigelow started stroking himself faster.

"Come over here, Elder," I said.

"Why?"

"I want you to shoot on my dick."

Elder Bigelow was too far gone by this point to resist and walked over the remaining distance to the shower. He shot onto my penis, and I used his semen as lubricant until I came, too.

"Oh, brother," he said. "Did we just have sex?"

I shook my head. "No, but all you have to do is say the word." I smiled at him.

"You perv."

I pulled the curtain closed and finished my shower. When I dried off and dressed, Elder Bigelow was sitting on the sofa looking very earnest. I walked to the kitchen and drank a glass of water, hoping my casual attitude would deescalate the situation.

"We have to talk about what happened," he said.

"You beat off and I beat off," I replied. "Don't tell me that's the first time you've beaten off on your mission."

He frowned. "Still," he said.

"I know why you're upset. It's Kevin, isn't it?" Kevin was an inactive member of the Church who we were trying to reactivate. Only Kevin had admitted a few nights ago to being gay, and Elder Bigelow was at a loss on how to proceed.

"You see what kind of life he leads," Elder Bigelow said. "Do you want to end up like that?"

"With a six-pack and guys calling at every hour of the day and night?"

Elder Bigelow was still frowning. "He'll have his day in the sun," he said, "and then he'll have eternity in Outer Darkness."

"You can do a lot of interesting things in the dark." I remembered my trainer walking over to my bed in the middle of the night once and gently putting his hand on my crotch. I'd pretended to be asleep and never said anything about it. In fact, the following night, I claimed it was too hot and slept without my garments.

Normally, a good Mormon would protest such a thing, but my trainer said nothing. A couple of hours later, I heard my companion kneel down beside my bed for several minutes while he looked. After that, though, I stopped making myself available to him. I was afraid I was encouraging him to behave inappropriately and without his consent.

"I'm going to have to report you, Elder Mortenson." My companion looked like he'd just dropped his ice cream cone in the street. "I *have* to," Elder Bigelow explained. "If it ever gets out that I knew and didn't say anything, *I'll* be sent home in disgrace."

That was exactly where I hadn't wanted this conversation to go. My parents had made it clear they'd only pay for my education if I attended BYU, and they would only pay for BYU if I completed an honorable mission.

Hence, the straight porn magazines.

"If I can get Kevin to repent, will you keep my secret?" I asked.

Elder Bigelow adjusted his glasses. "Let's see what you can do before I commit."

I phoned Kevin right then and asked if my companion and I could come over this evening. "Well, I'm kind of busy."

"It's important."

"I'm not coming back to church."

"If you don't let us come over, Elder Bigelow is going to tell our mission president I'm gay."

There was silence on the other end of the line for a moment. "*Are* you gay?" Kevin asked.

"If you let us come over tonight, I'll tell you," I replied.

I heard a chuckle over the line. "Boy, they sure teach you guys good sales techniques," he said.

"So what time shall we be there?"

"Is 7:00 good?"

"Only if you haven't served yourself dinner yet."

Elder Bigelow and I ate beef Stroganoff at Kevin's. My companion looked steadily at his plate while I kept glancing at Kevin's loose bangs and deeply tan skin. Though Kevin kept pressuring me throughout the meal to tell him if I was gay, I insisted on putting off the revelation until dessert. Then, while he was squirting Reddi-Wip onto pieces of apple pie, I told him about Elder Bigelow shooting onto my dick in the shower.

The whipped cream spewed across the counter.

"So I'm gay," I concluded, "but my companion isn't. And now he wants to tell on me."

Kevin's eyebrows furrowed, and he rubbed Elder Bigelow on the shoulder. Elder Bigelow brushed him off. "Dude, tattling isn't cool," said Kevin. "You'll ruin his life."

"Being gay will ruin his life."

Kevin made a face like *The Scream*, clapping both hands to either side of his head, and teetered back and forth like a metronome. The odd movement gained my companion's attention.

"Elder," said Kevin, "I've paid off all my student loans, bought this condo, and have that nice Alfa Romeo Spider out front." He motioned with his arms to indicate the expanse of his empire.

Elder Bigelow frowned at me and then turned back to Kevin. "That's hardly because you're gay. You're just…you're just smart or something."

Kevin laughed. "It's possible to be both," he admitted. "But you're wrong. I do have all this money because I'm gay."

He let the words hang in the air until we began to feel their weight. I was the first to speak. "The only way you can have money *because* you're gay is to be an escort…" Kevin shook his head. "…have a sugar daddy…" Kevin indicated no again. "…or be a porn star." Kevin didn't say anything.

"Oh, my heck!" Elder Bigelow gasped. "You're a porn star?"

"Well, I wouldn't say *star*," he said, feigning innocence, which he didn't do very well. "After the first few DVDs, I moved into filming and distribution." He smiled. "It helped that I was a Marketing major."

"Can we see one of the films you made?" I asked.

"Elder Mortenson!"

"Oh, calm down, buddy. You can sit in the bathroom and wait till it's over."

He scowled at me.

Kevin slipped a DVD into his player while I moved to the sofa. Elder Bigelow insisted on remaining in the living room to "make sure" Kevin and I didn't "get into trouble." The film was pretty damn good, and halfway through, I unzipped and started stroking myself. Elder Bigelow looked disgusted through most of the movie, but by the end, he'd unzipped, too. We both ended up with a handful of cum.

When Kevin turned the lights back on, I stood up, holding my hand out, and said, "If you'll excuse me…" I started to head toward the bathroom, but Kevin grabbed me around the waist and pulled me close, putting my hand to his lips and licking it clean.

"Oh my god!" Elder Bigelow tried to run past us to the bathroom himself. But Kevin caught him as well and licked his hand, too. "I've had sex *twice* today!" Elder Bigelow bawled. "I'm going to hell for sure!" He started sniffling, staring at his wet hand. "I'm going to be sent home. I'm going to be excommunicated. My parents won't pay for my schooling. I was supposed to go to MIT."

Kevin led us both back to the sofa, and we all sat down, Kevin in the middle. "Now, I think I have a solution for that," he said.

"I don't want to hear it," Elder Bigelow said.

"I do." I held my palm to my nose and could still detect the faint odor of sex.

Kevin then explained that he was looking for some new actors, and there was a market not only for Mormon porn but specifically Mormon missionary porn. "Of course, most of the actors in any of these movies aren't really Mormon, but I've always preferred authenticity when I could get it."

Elder Bigelow moaned loudly.

"I understand you guys have to keep up appearances, but on Preparation Day, you can come over here, and we can make some films." He smiled. "Lots of films. You get paid up front, you get royalties, and if the movies are a success, I can help you both through school. You won't be dependent on your parents."

"We'll be dependent on *you*," Elder Bigelow moaned.

"You'll be dependent on yourselves," Kevin corrected. He walked off to let us discuss the offer, but of course Elder Bigelow put his fingers in his ears when I attempted to say anything. I already knew I wanted to participate, whether I was paid or not, whether I was able to go to school or not. It was time to accept myself, whatever the consequences.

"I'm not gay, I'm not gay, I'm not gay," my companion kept chanting over and over again.

"Haven't you ever heard the term 'gay for pay'?" I asked.

"No."

"Kevin," I said, "I'll do it. We'll let you know tomorrow about Elder Bigelow."

"I'm not gay, I'm not gay, I'm not gay."

"You boys have a good evening." Kevin gave me a kiss and patted Elder Bigelow on the shoulder.

Back in our apartment, I put my companion to bed, turning on his electric blanket even though it was mid-August. He was still shivering, though, so I slid into bed beside him. "No," he said. "No."

"I'm not going to molest you," I said. "I just want to hold you." I put my arms around him, and he buried his face in my chest and cried.

"There, there," I whispered. "There's nothing to be scared of."

"But I *am* scared," he said. "I am, I am, I am."

I held him until he fell asleep and continued holding him until he woke up in the morning. His eyes were puffy and red. I fixed him some toast while he took a shower, and I waited until he left the bathroom before I went in. When I came out and went back to the bedroom to put on my suit, Elder Bigelow was sitting on his bed stiffly, already dressed.

He was going to report me to the president.

"Elder…" I said.

He held up a hand. "I'm all clean," he said. "Let's go over and make a movie before I change my mind."

"But…what…?"

He shrugged. "I lied," he said. "I am gay."

"That doesn't mean you have to do porn."

He shrugged again. "One day I'll look back and regret this," he said. "But one day I'll look back and be glad, too."

"Okay," I said with a smile, "I'll give Kevin a call. Even though it's not P-Day."

Soon we were on our way over to Kevin's place. Elder Bigelow was chatty and animated the entire way. "We could do a movie called 'Missionaries Moan When Mounting.' I'm really good at moaning." He tapped his thighs like he was playing the drums. "Or how about this? Two missionaries knock on someone's door, and when the man answers, one of them asks, 'Can We Cum Inside?'" He laughed. "Get it? Get it? That can be the title."

I was beginning to understand how Victor Frankenstein felt.

Later that morning, we shot some scenes for our first film. The next day, we skipped our morning proselytizing again and filmed a few more scenes. We went to the bank and opened new accounts that our parents and the Church didn't know about and deposited the money there. I handed a homeless man a few dollars as we headed back to our apartment.

Knowing how life worked, things probably wouldn't turn out as rosy as Kevin had suggested, despite his own luck.

But I wasn't sure that mattered. I was making love to my companion every day for a couple of hours, recording it for posterity, and getting paid for it.

There was nothing quite like lying next to a man I loved all night long and waking up to see his smiling face just a few inches away from mine.

This mission might not be the best two years of my life, I realized, but it was a damn good start.

Books by Johnny Townsend

Thanks for reading! If you enjoyed this book, could you please take a few minutes to write a review online? Reviews are helpful both to me as an author and to other readers, so we'd all sincerely appreciate your writing one! And if you did enjoy the book, here are some others I've written you might want to look up:

Mormon Underwear

Zombies for Jesus

A Gay Mormon Missionary in Pompeii

The Golem of Rabbi Loew

Marginal Mormons

Gay Gaslighting

Mormon Bullies

Going-Out-Of-Religion Sale

Escape from Zion

Gayrabian Nights

Missionaries Make the Best Companions

Invasion of the Spirit Snatchers

Sexual Solidarity

The Washing of Brains

Mormon Misfits

Interview with a Mission President

Sins of the Saints

The Last Days Linger

Mormon Madness

Out of the Missionary's Closet

Human Compassion for Beginners

Dead Mankind Walking

Breaking the Promise of the Promised Land

I Will, Through the Veil

Am I My Planet's Keeper?

Have Your Cum and Eat It, Too

Strangers with Benefits

Constructing Equity

Wake Up and Smell the Missionaries

Racism by Proxy

Orgy at the STD Clinic

Life Is Better with Love

Please Evacuate

Recommended Daily Humanity

The Camper Killings

Kinky Quilts: Patchwork Designs for Gay Men

Inferno in the French Quarter: The UpStairs Lounge Fire

Latter-Gay Saints: An Anthology of Gay Mormon Fiction (co-editor)

Available from your favorite online or neighborhood bookstore.

Wondering what some of those other books are about? Read on!

Invasion of the Spirit Snatchers

During the Apocalypse, a group of Mormon survivors in Hurricane, Utah gather in the home of the Relief Society president, telling stories to pass the time as they ration their food storage and await the Second Coming. But this is no ordinary group of Mormons—or perhaps it is. They are the faithful, feminist, gay, apostate, and repentant, all working together to help each other through the darkest days any of them have yet seen.

Gayrabian Nights

Gayrabian Nights is a twist on the well-known classic, *1001 Arabian Nights*, in which Scheherazade, under the threat of death if she ceases to captivate King Shahryar's attention, enchants him through a series of mysterious, adventurous, and romantic tales.

In this variation, a male escort, invited to the hotel room of a closeted, homophobic Mormon senator, learns that the man is poised to vote on a piece of anti-gay legislation the following morning. To prevent him from sleeping, so that the exhausted senator will miss casting his vote on the Senate floor, the escort entertains him with stories of homophobia, celibacy, mixed orientation marriages, reparative therapy, coming out, first love, gay marriage, and long-term successful gay relationships.

The escort crafts the stories to give the senator a crash course in gay culture and sensibilities, hoping to bring the man closer to accepting his own sexual orientation.

Inferno in the French Quarter: The UpStairs Lounge Fire

On Gay Pride Day in 1973, someone set the entrance to a French Quarter gay bar on fire. In the terrible inferno that followed, thirty-two people lost their lives, including a third of the local congregation of the Metropolitan Community Church, their pastor burning to death halfway out a second-story window as he tried to claw his way to freedom. A mother who'd gone to the bar with her two gay sons died alongside them. A man who'd helped his friend escape first was found dead near the fire escape. Two children waited outside a movie theater across town for a father and step-father who would never pick them up. During this era of rampant homophobia, several families refused to claim the bodies, and many churches refused to bury the dead. Author Johnny Townsend pored through old records and tracked down survivors of the fire as well as relatives and friends of those killed to compile this fascinating account of a forgotten moment in gay history.

A Gay Mormon Missionary in Pompeii

What is a gay Mormon missionary doing in Italy? He is trying to save his own soul as well as the souls of others. In these tales chronicling the two-year mission of Robert Anderson, we see a young man tormented by his inability to be the man the Church says he should be. In addition to his personal hell, Anderson faces a major earthquake, organized crime, a serious bus accident, and much more. He copes with horrendous mission leaders and his own suicidal tendencies. But one day, he meets another missionary who loves him, and his world changes forever.

Missionaries Make the Best Companions

What lies behind the freshly scrubbed façades of the Mormon missionaries we see about town? In these stories, an ex-Mormon tries to seduce a faithful elder by showing him increasingly suggestive movies. A sister missionary fulfills her community service requirement by babysitting for a prostitute. Two elders break their mission rules by venturing into the forbidden French Quarter. A senior missionary couple try to reactivate lapsed members while their own family falls apart back home. A young man hopes that serving a second full-time mission will lead him up the Church hierarchy. Two bored missionaries decide to make a little extra money moonlighting in a male stripper club. Two frustrated elders find an acceptable way to masturbate—by donating to a Fertility Clinic. A lonely man searches for the favorite companion he hasn't seen in thirty years.

The Golem of Rabbi Loew

Jacob and Esau Cohen are the closest of brothers. In fact, they're lovers. A doctor tries to combine canine genes with those of Jews, to improve their chances of surviving a hostile world. A Talmudic scholar dates an escort. A scientist tries to develop the "God spot" in the brains of his patients in hopes of creating a messiah.

A Jew-by-Choice navigates Jewish/Muslim relations during Pesach. A gay Lubavitcher dating a Catholic is attacked and left for dead but becomes a police officer in response. The Golem of Prague is really Rabbi Loew's secret lover.

While some of the Jews in Townsend's book are Orthodox, this collection of Jewish stories most certainly is not.

Am I My Planet's Keeper?

Global Warming. Climate Change. Climate Crisis. Climate Emergency. Whatever label we use, we are facing one of the greatest challenges to the survival of life as we know it.

But while addressing greenhouse gases is perhaps our most urgent need, it's not our only task. We must also address toxic waste, pollution, habitat destruction, and our other contributions to the world's sixth mass extinction event.

In order to do that, we must simultaneously address the unmet human needs that keep us distracted from deeper engagement in stabilizing our climate: moderating economic inequality, guaranteeing healthcare to all, and ensuring education for everyone.

And to accomplish *that*, we must unite to combat the monied forces that use fear, prejudice, and misinformation to manipulate us.

It's a daunting task. But success is our only option.

Wake Up and Smell the Missionaries

Two Mormon missionaries in Italy discover they share the same rare ability—both can emit pheromones on demand. At first, they playfully compete in the hills of Frascati to see who can tempt "investigators" most. But soon they're targeting each other non-stop.

Can two immature young men learn to control their "superpower" to live a normal life…and develop genuine love? Even as their relationship is threatened by the attentions of another man?

They seem just on the verge of success when a massive earthquake leaves them trapped under the rubble of their apartment in Castellammare.

With night falling and temperatures dropping, can they dig themselves out in time to save themselves? And will their injuries destroy the ability that brought them together in the first place?

Orgy at the STD Clinic

Todd Tillotson is struggling to move on after his husband is killed in a hit and run attack a year earlier during a Black Lives Matter protest in Seattle.

In this novel set entirely on public transportation, we watch as Todd, isolated throughout the pandemic, battles desperation in his attempt to safely reconnect with the world.

Will he find love again, even casual friendship, or will he simply end up another crazy old man on the bus?

Things don't look good until a man whose face he can't even see sits down beside him despite the raging variants.

And asks him a question that will change his life.

Please Evacuate

A gay, partygoing New Yorker unconcerned about the future or the unsustainability of capitalism is hit by a truck and thrust into a straight man's body half a continent away. As Hunter tries to figure out what's happening, he's caught up in another disaster, a wildfire sweeping through a Colorado community, the flames overtaking him and several schoolchildren as they flee.

When he awakens, Hunter finds himself in the body of yet another man, this time in northern Italy, a former missionary about to marry a young Mormon woman. Still piecing together this new reality, and beginning to embrace his latest identity, Hunter fights for his life in a devastating flash flood along with his wife *and* his new husband.

He's an aging worker in drought-stricken Texas, a nurse at an assisted living facility in the direct path of a hurricane, an advocate for the unhoused during a freak Seattle blizzard.

We watch as Hunter is plunged into life after life, finally recognizing the futility of only looking out for #1 and understanding the part he must play in addressing the global climate crisis…if he ever gets another chance.

Recommended Daily Humanity

A checklist of human rights must include basic housing, universal healthcare, equitable funding for public schools, and tuition-free college and vocational training.

In addition to the basics, though, we need much more to fully thrive. Subsidized childcare, universal pre-K, a universal basic income, subsidized high-speed internet, net neutrality, fare-free public transit (plus *more* public transit), and medically assisted death for the terminally ill who want it.

None of this will matter, though, if we neglect to address the rapidly worsening climate crisis.

Sound expensive? It is.

But not as expensive as refusing to implement these changes. The cost of climate disasters each year has grown to staggering figures. And the cost of social and political upheaval from not meeting the needs of suffering workers, families, and individuals may surpass even that.

It's best we understand that the vast sums required to enact meaningful change are an investment which will pay off not only in some indeterminate future but in fact almost immediately. And without these adjustments to our lifestyles and values, there may very well not be a future capable of sustaining freedom and democracy…or even civilization itself.

The Camper Killings

When a homeless man is found murdered a few blocks from Morgan Beylerian's house in south Seattle, everyone seems to consider the body just so much additional trash to be cleared from the neighborhood. But Morgan liked the guy. They used to chat when Morgan brought Nick groceries once a week.

And the brutal way the man was killed reminds Morgan of their shared Mormon heritage, back when the faithful agreed to have their throats slit if they ever revealed temple secrets.

Did Nick's former wife take action when her ex-husband refused to grant a temple divorce? Did his murder have something to do with the public accusations that brought an end to his promising career?

Morgan does his best to investigate when no one else seems to care, but it isn't easy as a man living paycheck to paycheck himself, only able to pursue his investigation via public transit.

As he continues his search for the killer, Morgan's friends withdraw and his husband threatens to leave. When another homeless man is killed and Morgan is accused of the crime, things look even bleaker.

But his troubles aren't over yet.

Will Morgan find the killer before the killer finds him?

What Readers Have Said

Townsend's stories are "a gay *Portnoy's Complaint* of Mormonism. Salacious, sweet, sad, insightful, insulting, religiously ethnic, quirky-faithful, and funny."

D. Michael Quinn, author of *The Mormon Hierarchy: Origins of Power*

"Told from a believably conversational first-person perspective, [*A Gay Mormon Missionary in Pompeii*'s] novelistic focus on Anderson's journey to thoughtful self-acceptance allows for greater character development than often seen in short stories, which makes this well-paced work rich and satisfying, and one of Townsend's strongest. An extremely important contribution to the field of Mormon fiction." Named to Kirkus Reviews' Best of 2011.

Kirkus Reviews

"The thirteen stories in *Mormon Underwear* capture this struggle [between Mormonism and homosexuality] with humor, sadness, insight, and sometimes shocking details....*Mormon Underwear* provides compelling stories, literally from the inside-out."

Niki D'Andrea, *Phoenix New Times*

"Townsend's lively writing style and engaging characters [in *Zombies for Jesus*] make for stories which force us to wake up, smell the (prohibited) coffee, and review our attitudes with regard to reading dogma so doggedly. These are tales which revel in the individual tics and quirks which make us human, Mormon or not, gay or not…"

A.J. Kirby, *The Short Review*

"The Rift," from *A Gay Mormon Missionary in Pompeii*, is a "fascinating tale of an untenable situation…a *tour de force*."

David Lenson, editor, *The Massachusetts Review*

"Pronouncing the Apostrophe," from *The Golem of Rabbi Loew*, is "quiet and revealing, an intriguing tale…"

Sima Rabinowitz, Literary Magazine Review, *NewPages.com*

The Circumcision of God is "a collection of short stories that consider the imperfect, silenced majority of Mormons, who may in fact be [the Church's] best hope….[The book leaves] readers regretting the church's willingness to marginalize those who best exemplify its ideals: those who love fiercely despite all obstacles, who brave challenges at great personal risk and who always choose the hard, higher road."

Kirkus Reviews

In *Mormon Fairy Tales*, Johnny Townsend displays "both a wicked sense of irony and a deep well of compassion."

Kel Munger, *Sacramento News and Review*

Zombies for Jesus is "eerie, erotic, and magical."

Publishers Weekly

"While [Townsend's] many touching vignettes draw deeply from Mormon mythology, history, spirituality and culture, [*Mormon Fairy Tales*] is neither a gaudy act of proselytism nor angry protest literature from an ex-believer. Like all good fiction, his stories are simply about the joys, the hopes and the sorrows of people."

Kirkus Reviews

"In *Inferno in the French Quarter* author Johnny Townsend restores this tragic event [the UpStairs Lounge fire] to its proper place in LGBT history and reminds us that the victims of the blaze were not just 'statistics,' but real people with real lives, families, and friends."

Jesse Monteagudo, *The Bilerico Project*

In *Inferno in the French Quarter*, "Townsend's heart-rending descriptions of the victims…seem to [make them] come alive once more."

Kit Van Cleave, *OutSmart Magazine*

Marginal Mormons is "an irreverent, honest look at life outside the mainstream Mormon Church….Throughout his musings on sin and forgiveness, Townsend beautifully demonstrates his characters' internal, perhaps irreconcilable struggles….Rather than anger and disdain, he offers an honest portrayal of people searching for meaning and community in their lives, regardless of their life choices or secrets." Named to Kirkus Reviews' Best of 2012.

Kirkus Reviews

The stories in *The Mormon Victorian Society* "register the new openness and confidence of gay life in the age of same-sex marriage….What hasn't changed is Townsend's wry, conversational prose, his subtle evocations of character and social dynamics, and his deadpan humor. His warm empathy still glows in this intimate yet clear-eyed engagement with Mormon theology and folkways. Funny, shrewd and finely wrought dissections of the awkward contradictions—and surprising harmonies—between conscience and desire." Named to Kirkus Reviews' Best of 2013.

Kirkus Reviews

"This collection of short stories [*The Mormon Victorian Society*] featuring gay Mormon characters slammed [me] in the face from the first page, wrestled my heart and mind to the floor, and left me panting and wanting more by the end. Johnny Townsend has created so many memorable characters in such few pages. I went weeks thinking about this book. It truly touched me."

Tom Webb, *A Bear on Books*

Dragons of the Book of Mormon is an "entertaining collection....Townsend's prose is sharp, clear, and easy to read, and his characters are well rendered..."

Publishers Weekly

"The pre-eminent documenter of alternative Mormon lifestyles...Townsend has a deep understanding of his characters, and his limpid prose, dry humor and well-grounded (occasionally magical) realism make their spiritual conundrums both compelling and entertaining. [*Dragons of the Book of Mormon* is] [a]nother of Townsend's critical but affectionate and absorbing tours of Mormon discontent." Named to Kirkus Reviews' Best of 2014.

Kirkus Reviews

In *Gayrabian Nights*, "Townsend's prose is always limpid and evocative, and…he finds real drama and emotional depth in the most ordinary of lives."

Kirkus Reviews

Gayrabian Nights is a "complex revelation of how seriously soul damaging the denial of the true self can be."

Ryan Rhodes, author of *Free Electricity*

Gayrabian Nights "was easily the most original book I've read all year. Funny, touching, topical, and thoroughly enjoyable."

Rainbow Awards

Lying for the Lord is "one of the most gripping books that I've picked up for quite a while. I love the author's writing style, alternately cynical, humorous, biting, scathing, poignant, and touching…. This is the third book of his that I've read, and all are equally engaging. These are stories that need to be told, and the author does it in just the right way."

Heidi Alsop, *Ex-Mormon Foundation Board Member*

In *Lying for the Lord*, Townsend "gets under the skin of his characters to reveal their complexity and conflicts....shrewd, evocative [and] wryly humorous."

Kirkus Reviews

In *Missionaries Make the Best Companions*, "the author treats the clash between religious dogma and liberal humanism with vivid realism, sly humor, and subtle feeling as his characters try to figure out their true missions in life. Another of Townsend's rich dissections of Mormon failures and uncertainties..." Named to Kirkus Reviews' Best of 2015.

Kirkus Reviews

In *Invasion of the Spirit Snatchers*, "Townsend, a confident and practiced storyteller, skewers the hypocrisies and eccentricities of his characters with precision and affection. The outlandish framing narrative is the most consistent source of shock and humor, but the stories do much to ground the reader in the world—or former world—of the characters....A funny, charming tale about a group of Mormons facing the end of the world."

Kirkus Reviews

"Townsend's collection [*The Washing of Brains*] once again displays his limpid, naturalistic prose, skillful narrative chops, and his subtle insights into psychology...Well-crafted dispatches on the clash between religion and self-fulfillment..."

Kirkus Reviews

"While the author is generally at his best when working as a satirist, there are some fine, understated touches in these tales [*The Last Days Linger*] that will likely affect readers in subtle ways....readers should come away impressed by the deep empathy he shows for all his characters—even the homophobic ones."

Kirkus Reviews

"Written in a conversational style that often uses stories and personal anecdotes to reveal larger truths, this immensely approachable book [*Racism by Proxy*] skillfully serves its intended audience of White readers grappling with complex questions regarding race, history, and identity. The author's frequent references to the Church of Jesus Christ of Latter-day Saints may be too niche for readers unfamiliar with its idiosyncrasies, but Townsend generally strikes a perfect balance of humor, introspection, and reasoned arguments that will engage even skeptical readers."

Kirkus Reviews

Orgy at the STD Clinic portrays "an all-too real scenario that Townsend skewers to wincingly accurate proportions...[with] instant classic moments courtesy of his punchy, sassy, sexy lead character..."

Jim Piechota, *Bay Area Reporter*

Orgy at the STD Clinic is "…a triumph of humane sensibility. A richly textured saga that brilliantly captures the fraying social fabric of contemporary life." Named to Kirkus Reviews' Best Indie Books of 2022.

Kirkus Reviews

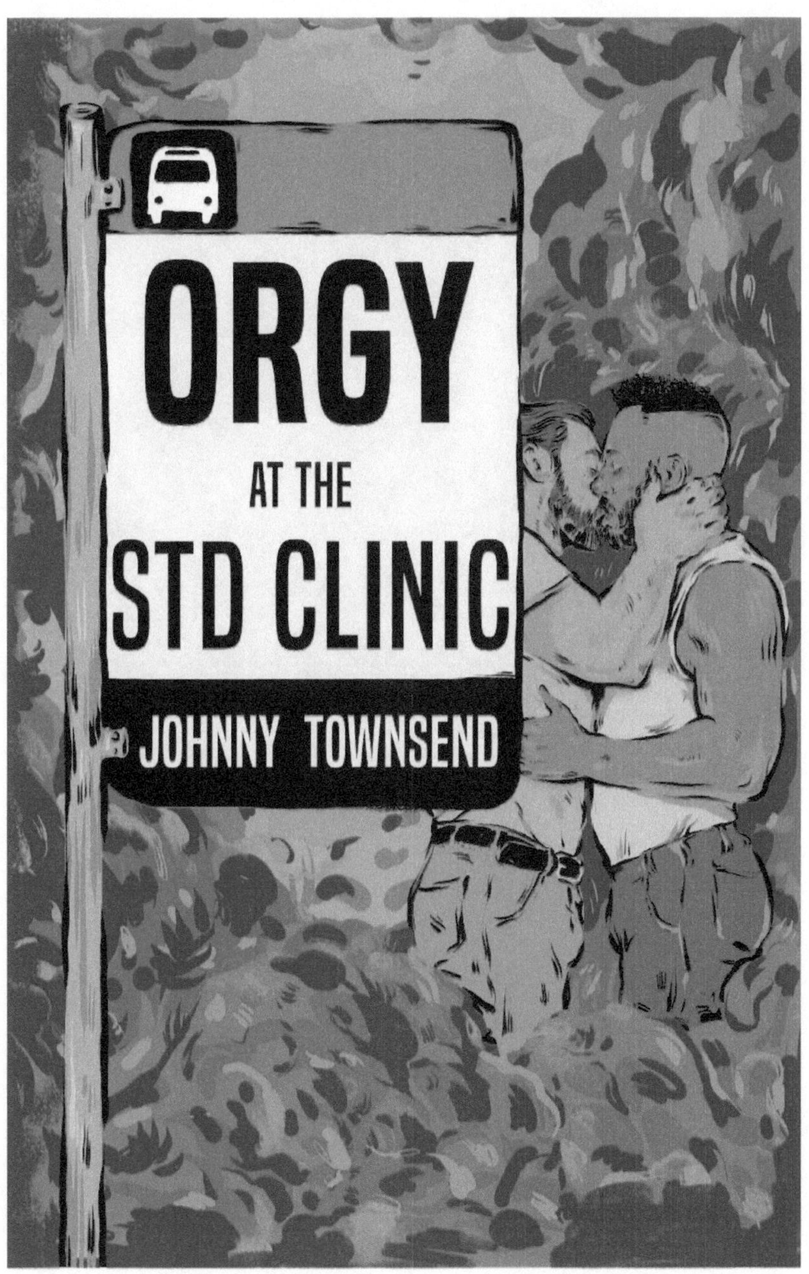

ORGY
AT THE
STD CLINIC
JOHNNY TOWNSEND

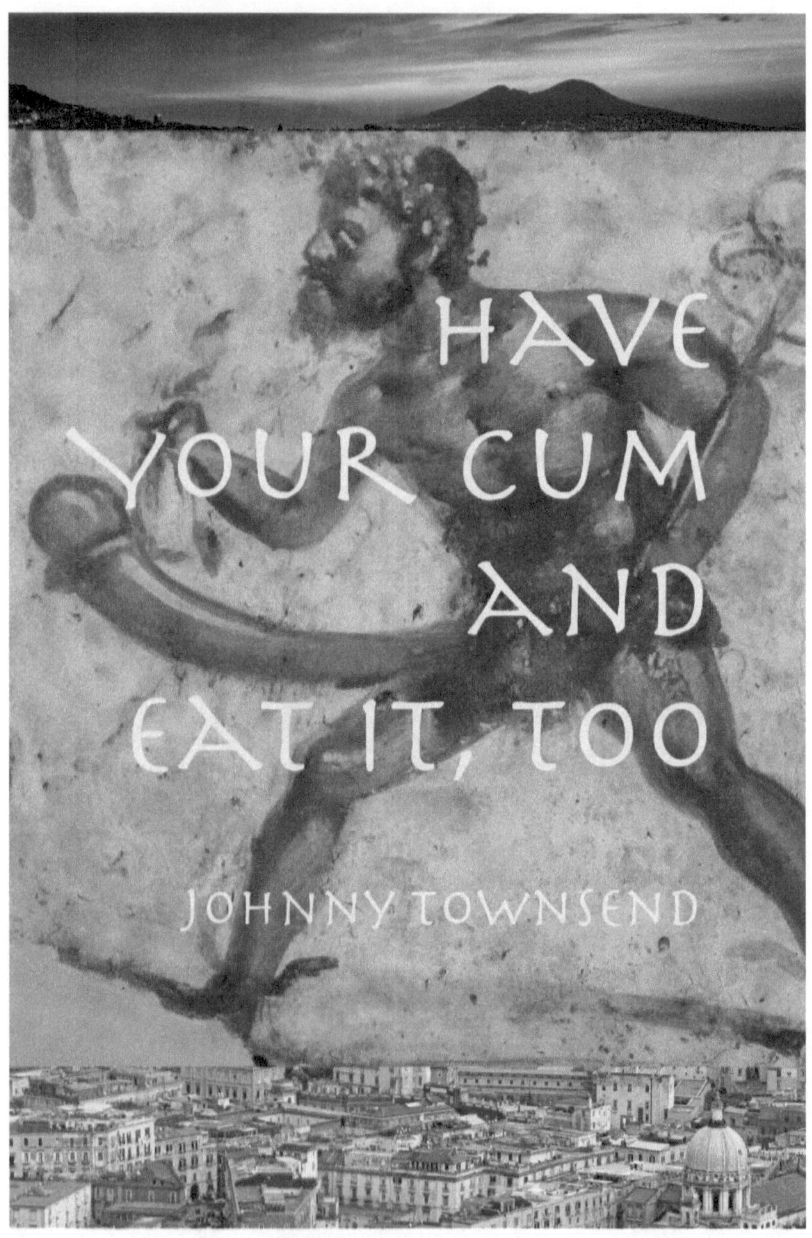
HAVE
YOUR CUM
AND
EAT IT, TOO
JOHNNY TOWNSEND

Going-Out-Of-
Religion Sale
JOHNNY TOWNSEND

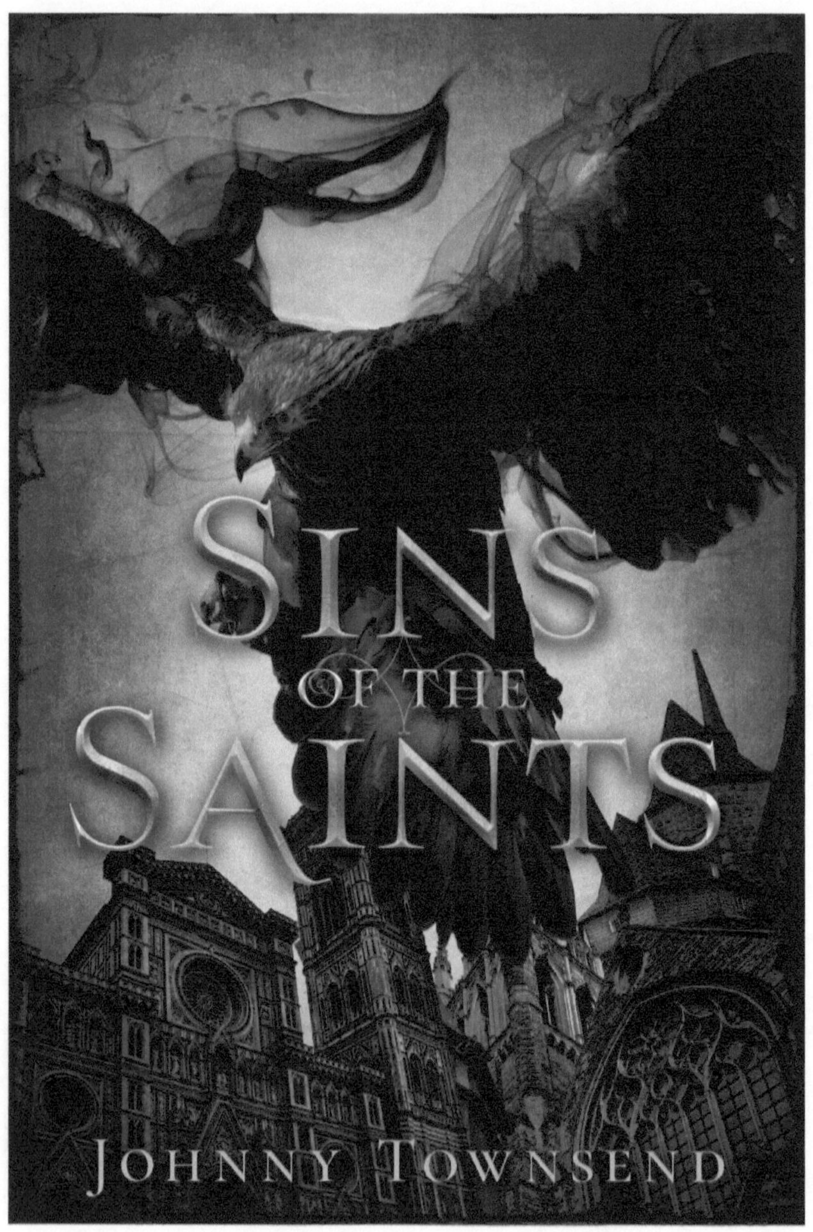

SINS
OF THE
SAINTS
JOHNNY TOWNSEND